JINGLE

GORDON KORMAN

Scholastic Press • New York

Library of Congress Cataloging-in-Publication Data available

ISBN 978-0-545-86142-7

10 9 8 7 6 5 4 3 2 1   16 17 18 19 20

Printed in the U.S.A.   23
First edition, October 2016

Book design by Elizabeth B. Parisi

For E. M. Baker School,
12 years. 3 Kormans. A million memories.

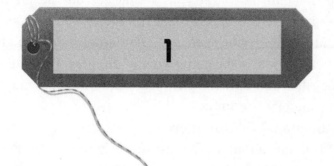

1

Dear Elf,

Thank you for volunteering to participate in Cedarville's annual Santa's Workshop Holiday Spectacular. As always, the festivities will be held at the Colchester mansion from December 18 through January 2.

Please report to the Mansion this weekend to be fitted for your elf costume. Don't forget to let us know of any special requirements, such as orthotic inserts for your pointed slippers.

Yuletide greetings!

The Colchester family

G riffin Bing reread the letter his best friend, Ben Slovak, held out to him. "'Dear Elf'? Why would the Colchesters make you an elf? Aren't you Jewish?"

"Half," Ben explained. "On my dad's side. We celebrate Hanukkah *and* Christmas. The point is, we don't celebrate either one by being an elf!"

Griffin shrugged. "It's obviously some kind of mistake. I mean, how did your name get on the elf list? Just write back and tell them thanks but no thanks."

"My mother won't let me," Ben lamented. "She grew up here. She's been going to the Holiday Spectacular since she was a little girl, just like you and me and everyone else we know."

"Bummer," Griffin offered.

"Tell me about it. Where am I going to fit Ferret Face in that tight little green vest? He's not a pet, you know. He's a medical service animal."

Hearing his name, the small weasel-like creature poked his head out from Ben's collar and looked around.

"Live it up now, Ferret Face," Ben advised darkly. "In a couple of weeks you'll be squeezed flat in an elf suit."

The creature withdrew back inside Ben's shirt.

"I feel sorry for you, Ben. When I'm at Santa's Workshop, I always pity those poor elves—dressed up like idiots with those pointy ears and bells on their shoes. But if your mom's forcing you, there's nothing you can do about it."

Ben's eyes had found a stack of mail on the Bings' kitchen counter. "Hey, that envelope's just like mine. Isn't that the Colchester family crest?"

In alarm, Griffin tore open the letter and stared at the contents.

Dear Elf . . .

"*Mom!!*" Griffin bellowed in a voice loud enough to bring Ferret Face to the surface again.

"I thought you said there's nothing we can do about it," put in Ben.

"There's nothing *you* can do about it," Griffin amended. "There's no way *I'm* going to dress up like a Brussels sprout and make a fool of myself in front of the whole town! *Mom!*"

No answer.

"I don't think she's here, Griffin."

"That's right—she's got jury duty. No problem, I'll take this to Dad. He's always got my back."

Mr. Bing's "office" was actually a workshop in the garage. He was a professional inventor, with several successful patents to his credit. Griffin punched in the code and the automatic door rose on an astounding sight.

A large orange globe hung suspended from the ceiling. Before it danced Griffin's father, armed with a golf club. He hacked at the metal surface, making loud clanging noises and yelling at the top of his lungs.

"Take that! And that! And that!"

"Why's he freaking out?" Ben asked in horror, patting the cowering Ferret Face inside the fabric of his T-shirt.

"It's his latest invention!" Griffin called back over the noise.

"What is it—an iron piñata?"

"Dad! Dad!" Griffin rushed up to his father, narrowly avoiding the swinging seven iron. "You don't have to wreck it! If it's no good, you can start over!"

Panting, Mr. Bing backed off and lowered the club. "Oh, hi, guys." Sweat poured down his face. "You're just in time."

"Why are you destroying all your hard work?" Griffin demanded.

"I'm not destroying it," his father replied, "I'm *testing* it. This is Fruit Armor. Every year, thousands of tons of pieces of fruit arrive at their destinations bruised and ruined during transportation. But with Fruit Armor, every delicate peach, apricot, or grape arrives in perfect condition. See?"

He opened the globe, which separated into two hemispheres. This revealed a slightly smaller inner globe made of rubberized plastic, protected by a system of springs and ball bearings. This he removed and placed on his worktable. It was full of apples—shiny, red, unmarked, and beautiful.

"These should be applesauce after what I've put them through," he announced proudly. "And look at them. They're perfect."

"Great, Dad." Griffin's mind was elsewhere. "Look at what came in the mail today. You've got to get me out of it."

His father read the elf letter. "You're so lucky! When I was your age, I'd have given my right arm to be an elf at Santa's Workshop!"

"I guess things were pretty different back when you were a kid," Ben offered.

"I'll never forget the thrill of walking into the Colchester mansion the first time," Mr. Bing reminisced. "I was four years old, and I thought I was in heaven! The size of the place . . . the decorations . . . the tree with that special star! Even today, when I think of the holidays, the first thing that comes to mind is Santa's Workshop."

Griffin watched his father's face grow more and more animated. This was not the reaction he'd been hoping for. "Come on, Dad, I kind of like it, too. What's not to like? But as a guest, not stuffed in green tights, wiping kids' noses while putting them on Santa's lap. They cry; they spill their juice. And if they barf, you have to clean it up!"

"Are you kidding?" crowed Mr. Bing. "Those elves were like rock stars to me. I used to look at them and think they had it made. Your mom was an elf back in high school. The first time I asked her out on a date she said no because she had elf duty."

Griffin's heart was sinking. Not Mom, too! How was he ever going to get out of this? "Well, congrats, Dad, on the, uh, Fruit Armor."

"I hope it's a big success," Ben added.

"Thanks," Mr. Bing acknowledged, looking pleased with himself. "I've got to get this prototype over to Daria Vader's. It's time to start the legal paperwork for the patent office."

As they stepped out behind the closing garage door,

the grinding gears of a big motor caught their attention. A transport truck roared past the Bing home. On its flatbed trailer lay a thick, dark green fir tree at least twenty-five feet long.

"That has to be going to the Colchesters'," Ben observed sourly. "Who else would order a Christmas tree that big?"

As the truck swept by, they both saw a smaller figure behind it, moving just as fast. Antonia "Pitch" Benson rollerbladed up the street and swooped onto the driveway, stopping on a dime in front of them. She was the best Rollerblader in town, and also the best at everything else athletic—including climbing. She was better at that than at all other sports combined.

Clutched in her gloved hand was an all-too-familiar envelope.

"Don't tell me you got a 'Dear Elf' letter, too!" Griffin blurted.

Pitch's face was a thundercloud. "Oh, it gets way better than that. My parents have already rescheduled our rock-climbing trip to Sedona so I won't miss this fabulous honor!"

Ben was bewildered. "That's three of us already."

"Four," Pitch amended. "Savannah got one yesterday. Her parents volunteered to take care of her animals so she can elf it up with us."

At that moment, Griffin's phone pinged. It was a text from their friend Melissa Dukakis: **If you get invited to be an elf, do you have to do it?**

Ben's eyes widened. "Melissa, too? That's all of us except Logan!"

Griffin dialed Logan's number. There was no answer.

"Let's go over there," Griffin decided. "How did our whole team get on the elf list?"

"It's a mystery," Pitch said grimly. "And I don't like mysteries."

"Logan's not going to like this, either," Ben commented as they started in the direction of the Kellerman house. "It'll take time away from his acting. Didn't he just join that theater company?"

Griffin shook his head. "He tried but he didn't get in. Poor guy was pretty broken up about it. You know how he is about his acting career."

"He's probably devastated," Ben agreed.

"He doesn't seem so devastated to me." Pitch pointed down the block toward the Kellerman home. There was their friend Logan.

Griffin squinted. "What's he doing? Is that *dancing*?"

Logan was in the front yard, hopping and skipping around the base of a small blue spruce, his arms alternately at his hips and up over his head.

"What gives, Kellerman?" called Pitch. "Why the Riverdance?"

"Oh, hey, guys," Logan greeted them. "I'm practicing my Christmas jig. How am I doing?"

"That depends," Ben told him. "If you're trying to be arrested, you've nailed it. What Christmas jig?"

"At the Holiday Spectacular," Logan explained, "all the elves perform a jig around the tree. You guys better start practicing, too, if we're going to have a polished performance."

Pitch's eyes narrowed. "How do you know that the rest of us are elves, too?"

"I'm the one who signed us up!"

"You *what*?" Griffin turned crimson. "Where would you get a crazy idea like that?"

"From *you*!"

"From me?" Griffin echoed. "I think I'd remember saying, 'Wouldn't it be great if Logan volunteered us all to be elves!'"

"When I got rejected by the North Shore Players, you said that instead of complaining, I should come up with a plan to get myself in. This is my plan. Yvette Boucle, the director of the Players, lives in Green Hollow, just one town away. Her daughter, Tiffany, is an elf every year. If I'm an elf, too, and really knock it out of the park, her mother will see what a great actor I am and change her mind about rejecting me."

"That's why *you* have to be an elf," Pitch said through clenched teeth. "Why do *we* have to do it?"

"Well, every star needs a supporting cast." Logan gave Griffin a dazzling smile. "I guess you're not the only Man With The Plan around here anymore."

Enraged, Pitch lunged at Logan. Only the frantic efforts of Griffin and Ben held her back from going for his throat.

"Kellerman, I'm missing Red Rocks because of you!"

Ferret Face poked his head out of Ben's sleeve, hissing vigorously, a sign of agitation.

"Calm down, everybody," Ben soothed, his shoulders slumped in resignation. "There's no point in getting all bent out of shape about this. However we ended up on elf duty, our parents are going to make us do it. They *love* the Holiday Spectacular. It's a tradition that we've been part of since before we could walk."

"Fine." Pitch looked daggers at Logan. "But you owe us, Kellerman. You owe us *huge*."

"And from now on," Griffin added, "all the plans around here come from *me*! Understood?"

Griffin Bing had always believed that nothing was impossible if you had the right plan. Now he saw how wrong that could be.

No plan could save a person from elf-hood.

2

The Colchester mansion was a magnificent stone home on a sprawling, hilly property overlooking the sparkling waters of Long Island Sound.

Melissa Dukakis agitated her head, causing her curtain of long, stringy hair to part, revealing beady black eyes. "Wow," she whispered. "I'd forgotten how awesome this place is."

Griffin nodded, taking in the sweeping balconies and elegant landscaping. "Maybe being an elf won't be so bad if we get to come here every day."

"They said we'll be done in an hour," Logan said into the open window of the Kellermans' van. "This is just a meet and greet, and to get us fitted for costumes." He took a deep breath. "I can smell the challenge of a new role."

"You're not going to smell anything with a broken nose," Pitch warned as Mr. Kellerman continued around the circular drive and roared off. "I haven't forgotten that this is all your fault."

"Chill out," Logan told her. "It's is going to be great. Everybody loves Santa's Workshop."

"I see one person who doesn't look like such a big fan," Ben commented with a motion of his head toward the property next door.

At the boundary fence, a sour-faced older woman stood at her mailbox, scowling in their direction.

Griffin snapped his fingers. "That must be Miss Grier. My folks told me about her. She's hated Santa's Workshop ever since *they* were kids—always complaining about the noise and the traffic and people parking all over the place. They called her Miss Grinch."

Miss Grier grabbed a handful of mail, tossed one more contemptuous look in the direction of the Colchester property, and stormed back to her home.

"Real neighborly, these rich people," put in Pitch.

A cardboard sign reading ELF REGISTRATION directed them toward a side entrance. They were almost at the door when a large SUV pulled up. Out stepped Savannah Drysdale, leading a Doberman pinscher the size of a small pony.

At the sight of the big dog, Ferret Face crawled up Ben's sleeve and cowered there. Luthor made the little creature nervous. Truth be told, Luthor made all of them nervous except Savannah. While she thought her "sweetie" was the gentlest, most harmless creature in the world, Griffin and the others remembered very well Luthor's old life as a guard dog. They knew how little it took for him to revert back to his ferocious former self.

"Why'd you bring the dog, Savannah?" Logan complained.

"We always do everything together on the weekend," Savannah explained.

"Why didn't you just tell him it's Wednesday?" asked Ben.

"Because he knows. He counts the school days. Besides, I would never lie to Luthor."

"He better not cause trouble," Logan warned. "Remember, Tiffany Boucle is an elf, too. If my friend's dog trashes Santa's Workshop, I'll never get into the North Shore Players."

Savannah's expression hardened. "Luthor is as gentle as a kitten." To emphasize that the subject was closed, she led the big Doberman down the cobblestone path to the side of the stately home. The others followed.

They arrived at a door that was less grandiose than the mansion's main portal, but still impressive—a heavy oak panel studded in brass. It was the service entrance, and beneath that sign was a hand-lettered cardboard one that read, WELCOME ELVES.

It drew a low moan from Ben. "I know that's what we are, but do they have to keep rubbing it in?"

"There are no small roles," Logan lectured him. "Only small actors."

The door opened before Griffin could knock, and a tall, haughty gentleman appeared on the stoop. "The elves, I presume?" His accent was British, his suit black and impeccably tailored, his long nose turned up as if he smelled something bad.

"My name is Priddle. I am Mr. Colchester's personal secretary." The eyes looking down that nose were cold as ice, and they fell next on Luthor. "The animal must remain outside, of course."

"Luthor is as much a part of this group as I am," pleaded Savannah, shocked.

"Then you will remain outside as well," said Priddle without hesitation.

A protest died on Savannah's lips. The Colchesters were the most beloved family in the history of Cedarville. If she threw a fit and refused to participate, her parents would only send her back again, this time without her loving companion.

"It's okay, sweetie," she murmured to the big dog, wrapping the leash around a downspout. "I won't be long. Be a good boy."

Priddle matched their names to a master list and then led them down a long corridor into an area of changing rooms off the indoor pool. "Girls to the left, boys to the right. Choose a costume of your size and put it on."

The elf costumes included a leather jerkin over a green tunic, tights, long-toed shoes with bells on the end, pointy ear attachments, and a beanie with red pom-poms. The six friends stepped from behind the curtains at the same time. The embarrassment was balanced by the fact that everybody else was in the same absurd outfit. There were a few nervous giggles, but no teasing or belly laughs.

Logan had the only criticism. "You look great, but you're too serious. You have to smile. Elves are *happy*."

"Not the ones who got cheated out of climbing at Red Rocks," Pitch put in sourly.

Priddle looked them over. "Quite acceptable. This way, please."

The next stop was the Great Hall, the largest space in the mansion, with its soaring ceiling. Workmen were already constructing the indoor castle that would house Santa's throne, and the Workshop, where the little kids could string popcorn and decorate gingerbread men. The sight of it brought back happy memories of visits here as younger children.

Between the twin staircases rose the Christmas tree, stretching a full twenty-five feet in the air. At its peak gleamed the Star of Prague, a priceless heirloom that was considered to be the most valuable item anywhere in Cedarville. It was a large crystal orb that housed a magnificent five-pointed star made of multi-colored stained glass. The translucent outer globe was newer, but the original Star dated back to the tenth century, when it had been owned by Saint Wenceslaus himself.

At the base of the tree was another elf. She could almost have been the real thing as she tilted her head to gaze up at the Star.

"Is it just me," Ben whispered to Griffin, "or does an elf getup actually suit her?"

She was petite, with honey-colored hair cascading from her slouchy cap. Even the plastic points on her ears somehow completed her heart-shaped face.

Melissa moved her curtain of hair aside for a better view. "So that's how it's supposed to look."

"It's her!" hissed Logan. "It's Tiffany Boucle!"

"The girl whose mom kicked you out of the North Shore Players?" asked Savannah.

Logan squared his shoulders and adjusted his jerkin. "Are my ears on straight?"

"Perfectly," Pitch assured him. "It's the rest of your head you should be worried about."

"Hilarious," Logan said sarcastically. "My whole acting career is riding on this, and you're cracking jokes."

Even Ferret Face watched with interest as Logan crossed the Great Hall to the base of the huge tree. The bells on his shoes jingled as he tripped over a thick black cable. If the electrician hadn't grabbed his arm to steady him, it would have been a total wipeout.

"What are all these wires doing on the floor?" Logan demanded.

The middle-aged man shrugged. "It takes a lot of power to run the Workshop, son. We've got animatronic reindeer, toy soldiers and drummer boys, a miniature train, not to mention floodlights, spotlights, and Christmas lights. The tree alone has over twenty thousand bulbs. A two-hundred-year-old mansion wasn't built to handle this kind of juice."

At last, Logan made his way over to the girl who wore the green-and-tan costume so naturally and with such grace. She was gazing up at the Star of Prague, which sparkled in the sun streaming in through the windows. That might have explained why she didn't notice him—not even when he cleared his throat loudly.

This didn't bother Logan. He was an actor, trained in ad lib—the ability to improvise when a performance wasn't going as planned.

"Great star, huh?" he said to her. "Pretty tight."

Okay, it wasn't as creative as he was hoping for, but it got the job done. At least she realized he was there.

"I know," she told him. "My mom's an art history professor. She's fascinated with it."

"I thought your mom was the director of the North Shore Players," Logan blurted in surprise.

"That's just part-time," Tiffany explained. "Her day job is teaching at the community college. She's dying to finish her book about the Star, but the Colchesters won't give her access to it. They don't want it to get too famous. They'd rather keep it a Cedarville holiday tradition, not some world-renowned treasure that draws visitors from all over."

"That's really interesting," said Logan, stifling a yawn. He needed a way to steer the conversation back to the North Shore Players. "Traditions are important. That's why I wanted to be an elf. A lot of people think all you have to do is put on a costume. But it takes a lot of acting ability to bring depth to the role."

She frowned. "Depth?"

"Of course," Logan enthused. "For example, what's my character's motivation? How's my relationship with Santa? How do I feel about my place in the toy-making supply chain? Am I resentful because other elves were promoted ahead of me . . . ?"

Logan was just warming up to the subject when a booming laugh interrupted him.

"Where'd you get the costumes, you guys?" came the obnoxious voice of Darren Vader. "Did Tinker Bell have a garage sale?"

3

It drew a giggle from Tiffany, and she craned her neck to find the source of the comment.

Into the Great Hall strutted big Darren, a leering grin on his broad face. His eyes panned the group, coming to rest on Griffin, his archenemy. "Nice tights, Bing."

"What are you doing here, Vader?" Griffin growled.

"Same as you," Darren shot back. "Getting my elf on."

Tiffany laughed again. In alarm, Logan noted that she was regarding Darren with admiration.

"No way, Darren!" Logan exclaimed. "You've never volunteered for anything in your life!"

"That's mean!" Tiffany accused.

"I take that personally, Kellerman," Darren announced. "I'm so community-minded that 'Cedarville' comes up in my alphabet soup."

"Real smart making fun of our costumes when you're going to be wearing the same thing," Pitch said.

"Assuming they can find tights in size a thousand," added Griffin with relish.

"Ha!" Darren snorted a laugh. "Nice one, Bing."

Tiffany rushed over to shake hands with Darren. "I'm Tiffany Boucle. I think it's great that we're going to be elves together."

Logan was crushed. Tiffany hadn't bothered to introduce herself to *him*.

"Darren Vader," the big boy told her grandly. "Welcome to Cedarville."

Logan sidled up to Griffin. "Like he's the mayor or something," he muttered under his breath.

"I wonder what Vader's *really* doing here," Griffin mused as Darren and Tiffany got acquainted. "There's no way that money-grubber would volunteer for elf duty if there wasn't something in it for him."

At that moment, all activity ceased in the Great Hall. Even the workmen dropped what they were doing and stood up in respect. Charles Colchester, Cedarville's most illustrious citizen, surveyed what would soon be the sixty-sixth annual Santa's Workshop. He was a very tall, distinguished-looking gentleman with military stature and iron-gray hair and mustache. His hand was on the shoulder of a middle-school boy with tousled blond locks and the kind of deep suntan that no Long Islander had this time of year.

Priddle rushed across the Great Hall to greet his employer. "Mr. Colchester, may I present this year's elves."

Mr. Colchester grinned broadly, which instantly made him appear twenty years younger, kind and friendly. "Thanks for coming, kids. It means a lot to my family that we can continue to do this year after year. And I've brought you one more elf—all the way from California. This is my grandson, Russell."

Russell shared zero of his grandfather's charm. "Hi," he announced in a voice that lacked any interest or enthusiasm.

"Well, I'll leave you all to get acquainted. Russell, I'll see you at dinner. Have fun."

Cedarville's most renowned host left the Great Hall.

Tiffany was in the middle of a sentence, but Darren turned his back on her and walked over to Russell Colchester. "Great to meet you, Russ. I'm Darren. Let me guess—you're not too thrilled about flying three thousand miles to squeeze your buns into green elf tights."

Russell smiled at Darren in spite of himself. "Am I that obvious?"

"I can already tell the two of us think alike," Darren said confidentially. "Don't worry. You don't have to rock the leprechaun suit. You just have to look better than Slovak over there. He's the shrimpy one with the toothpick legs and the weasel sticking out of his collar."

Russell did a double take. "Is that a rat?"

Ben drew himself up to his full height, which wasn't very tall. "He's a ferret, and he's a trained service animal. I have narcolepsy, and it's his job to bite me if I start to fall asleep."

Russell turned back to Darren. "Is he serious?"

"I don't get it, either," Darren admitted. "Kids are weird around here, Russ. Lucky you found me."

"Follow me, you two," Priddle instructed Russell and Darren. "We'll see about your costumes." He led them off in the direction of the changing rooms.

"Well, now we know why Vader signed up for elf duty," Pitch concluded. "He's here to suck up to the rich kid."

"The Vaders are pretty rich, too," commented Melissa from behind her hair.

"Not Colchester rich," Griffin countered.

Ben was insulted. "I don't care if he has a trillion dollars. It doesn't give him the right to call Ferret Face a rat."

Savannah was always ready to stick up for animals. "There's nothing wrong with rats."

"I know we're all supposed to love the Colchesters," Pitch observed, "but this kid Russell seems like kind of a jerk. And if he starts palling around with Vader, that would be jerk squared."

Tiffany spoke up. "I don't get what everybody has against Darren. He's so funny. Maybe you're just misunderstanding his sense of humor."

Griffin was serious. "Listen, Tiffany. You didn't grow up in Cedarville. We've all got plenty of history with Darren, and none of it's funny."

She was about to give him an argument, but she was cut off by the roar of a backfiring engine so loud that it penetrated deep inside the huge mansion.

"Is that a *motorcycle*?" Ben shouted over the noise.

The engine died abruptly to be replaced by thunderous barking that could only be coming from one source.

"Luthor!" breathed Savannah.

This was followed by the sound of heavy leather boots on the polished oak floors. Nervous glances passed between the elves, and all eyes turned to the door leading from the service entrance.

The footsteps grew closer—like a gunfighter striding into a saloon in the Old West.

The door was thrown open so violently that it swung around and bashed the paneled wall. In walked a bear of a man wrapped in a nail-studded black leather jacket and ripped jeans. He was so large that Luthor looked normal size alongside him. The barking had stopped, and the big dog rubbed submissively up against the newcomer's denim-clad legs. A broken section of drainpipe dangled from the looped end of his leash.

Who was this monster who had conquered Luthor and obviously had no business being anywhere near the gracious Colchester mansion? The elves cowered before him, and even the workmen paused in their tasks to look on in concern. Everybody was struck dumb—all except the last person anyone expected to sound the alarm.

"Mr. Priddle!" shrilled Melissa, way beyond her top volume. "Mr. Priddle, come quick!"

The secretary rushed into the Great Hall. "What is it? What's wrong?"

The elves stared at him. Couldn't he see that a giant biker had stormed the mansion?

"Oh, I see now," Priddle exclaimed in consternation. "The dog got in. And he's broken the drainpipe!"

"Not the *dog*!" Ben shouted. "The *guy*!"

"Oh," the secretary said in sudden understanding. "May I present Mr. Dirk Crenshaw. He'll be our Santa Claus at the Holiday Spectacular."

Dead silence. No one in the history of the world had ever looked less like Jolly Old Saint Nick than this wild-eyed hulk four times the size of any of them. He would have fit in better in a gang war than in a Christmas party.

"Santa," Priddle went on, "these are your elves."

In greeting, Crenshaw opened his mouth wide enough to drive a truck through and emitted a long, rolling belch that smelled of garlic and stale cigars.

"We'd better watch out," Pitch mumbled under her breath.

Griffin understood her meaning instantly. Santa Claus had come to town.

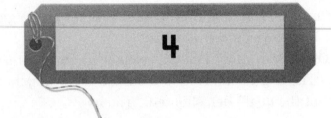

4

Quit scratching, Ferret Face."

Ben pulled on the green fabric in an attempt to make space inside the tight shirt. It was no use. Elf suits were not made with ferrets in mind.

In the bedroom mirror, Ben could see the bump under his shirt wriggling like mad as the little creature struggled to find a comfortable position. "You'll just have to get used to it," Ben said sternly. "I don't like it any more than you do. It's only for a couple of weeks. Let's go get some pepperoni."

Hearing the name of his favorite breakfast, Ferret Face decided to settle down. The little animal was the lucky one, Ben decided. He only had to deal with the squeezy shirt. The squeezy pants were the real problem. Ben was pretty sure he was walking like a stick insect all the way down the stairs. Or maybe that was just his cautious gait to keep his ear points from falling off.

On the way to the kitchen, he paused at the foot of the stairs, taking in the small display that stood there—a tabletop Christmas tree beside a Hanukkah menorah. It looked pretty dinky in comparison with the giant fir tree at Santa's Workshop, capped by the magnificent Star of Prague. Then again, the Slovak house wasn't exactly the Colchester mansion, either. Besides, Ben's family always had to split their celebration between the two holidays.

"Oh, Benjamin, you look adorable!" Mrs. Slovak exclaimed as her son came into the kitchen.

"I look like a garden gnome with bony knees."

His father laughed. "Suck it up, kid. You're part of a Cedarville tradition."

"I should sue Logan Kellerman for getting me into this," Ben muttered, pushing a slice of pepperoni through the tight shirt down to Ferret Face's eager mouth. It served Logan right that the girl he was trying to impress seemed to be developing a crush on Darren Vader, of all people. Yuck.

After breakfast, Mr. Slovak drove Ben to the mansion, steering carefully around the orange traffic cones set out by Miss Grier.

"Same old Miss Grinch, I see," Dad commented. "Still determined that no one should be allowed to trespass on her property."

"If you think she's bad, wait till you get a load of Santa. Little kids are going to run a mile before climbing on *his* lap." Ben stepped carefully out of the car, jingling all the way. "I'll be late today. We've got our first full rehearsal."

In spite of himself, Ben had to admit that Santa's Workshop looked amazing. The indoor castle was complete, and the activity booths were set up and decorated with sprayed-on snow. Large light-up flakes dangled everywhere, and Mr. O'Bannon, the electrician, bustled from station to station, repairing loose wires with a soldering gun.

"Not so fast! Not so fast!" he exclaimed in agitation. "Don't power them all up at the same time! The wiring in this old building can't handle it!"

"You say the same thing every year," Priddle reminded him. "And every year this old building manages just fine."

The Holiday Spectacular's elves were nowhere near ready for opening night, which was only four days away. The Christmas jig was a disaster. The costumes were too tight to allow for easy movement. Griffin had two left feet, and Darren had no feet at all—none that he was willing to move, anyway. Pitch, who was the best athlete in town, had the ability but not the grace. And Russell refused to dance, period.

"Grandpa can drag me here and force me to put on the costume. But that's where it ends."

"I'm with you, Russ," Darren told him supportively. "Fight the power."

Ferret Face, who suffered from motion sickness, spit up inside Ben's elf suit. It made the merely uncomfortable now unbearable.

"Where do you think you're going?" demanded Priddle as Ben tried to slink off to the bathroom.

"I just need to—wash up a little." Ben decided not to go into the details of the ferret barf trickling down his chest.

"Not now," the secretary ordered. "We're just about to practice our caroling."

Singing carols was another responsibility that came with the elf gig. Never mind that Ben had to kneel in the front row, trying not to yelp while Darren delivered kick after kick from behind. The organist was Yvette Boucle, Tiffany's mother. Logan was so determined to capture her attention that he sang too loud and stood too far forward, staring at her.

"If he wants to make a good impression," Griffin whispered to Ben, "why does he look like he's trying to inhale the sheet music?"

Ben didn't answer. Ferret barf took all the zest out of a guy.

Tiffany sang a solo, and she was really good, her clear soprano soaring up to the Star of Prague. Everyone applauded except sour-faced Russell. Determined to score points with her mother, Logan ran up to high-five Tiffany. But she was looking for Darren's approval, and ducked under Logan's reaching arm. He ended up delivering a solid wallop to the back of the organist's head, knocking her off the piano bench.

"Sorry," Logan said as he helped her up off the floor. "I hope this doesn't affect my chances of getting into the North Shore Players."

"It won't," she assured him, trying to straighten her skirt. "You had a zero percent chance before, and that hasn't changed at all."

But the worst part of being an elf was Santa himself. Nobody expected a hired Santa Claus to be the real thing, but Crenshaw was remarkably unfriendly and spoke only when he had to, in single-syllable grunts. He smelled of cigars and oil and gas fumes from his ancient motorcycle. He took constant smoke breaks outside on the grounds, where he was visited by friends who looked exactly like he did—black-jacketed bikers. The roar of Harley-Davidson engines regularly interrupted rehearsals.

"Where did they find this guy—Mount Doom?" Pitch wondered aloud.

Melissa parted her curtain of hair to reveal eyes that were even more haunted than usual. "Isn't Santa supposed to be jolly? He's not jolly; he's mean."

"And his *friends*," Griffin added. "They're as bad as he is! You know what they all call him? *Fingers!* That's a nickname for a crook, not a Santa Claus!"

"I overheard them talking about losing money betting on horses," Ben put in. "That's why he took this job—to pay off his gambling debts!"

"Job!" Logan was bitter for a different reason. "Dirk

Crenshaw has an acting job, and I can't even get into the North Shore Players. Where's the justice in that?"

"Maybe it wasn't such a smooth move to punch the director," Pitch suggested drily.

"I refuse to listen to any of this," Savannah said stubbornly. "Sure, Dirk is a little rough around the edges. But he must be a good person inside."

The others stared at her.

"Why?" Melissa ventured.

"Isn't it obvious? Luthor *loves* him. Animals are always better judges of character than people."

It was true. The big Doberman had a special affection for the gruff and rude Santa, following him like an adoring puppy. For his part, Crenshaw didn't exactly return Luthor's feelings, but he seemed to tolerate the giant dog licking his hands and frolicking around his studded biker boots.

"Luthor doesn't love him," Griffin argued. "Luthor's afraid of him, too."

"That's even worse!" Ben insisted. "If that guy scares an apex predator like Luthor, then we've got the Terminator for a Santa Claus!"

Savannah rolled her eyes. "Now you're just being ridiculous. You can't judge a book by its cover, you know. And you've got to admit that when he gets in costume, Dirk is the *perfect* Santa."

That was the strangest part of all. The instant "Fingers" Crenshaw put on his red-and-white suit and white beard, he was transformed. The ill-tempered, unfriendly, cigar-smoking biker became the ultimate Saint Nicholas. The reddish complexion of someone who was perpetually ticked off became jolly with rosy cheeks. And the burly bulk of a professional thug turned into Santa's famous jelly belly.

"Okay, so he looks the part," Ben conceded. "Blood looks like cherry syrup, too. That doesn't mean I want it on my ice cream."

Ferret Face stuck his head inquisitively out of Ben's jerkin. In the Slovak home, ice cream was usually served after pizza, and pizza meant pepperoni might be available.

"You're wrong," Savannah said firmly. "And anyway, it's thanks to him that Luthor is welcome in the mansion. I couldn't stand the thought of him tied up outside like a—like a—"

"Like an animal?" Pitch suggested helpfully.

"Like an outcast," Savannah finished. "And now he's not only allowed inside, he's part of Santa's Workshop."

Luthor was so attached to the hired Santa that removing him from the Great Hall had become a nightmare, despite Savannah's renowned dog-whispering skills. Outside, the big Doberman had taken to howling so loud that rehearsal was impossible. His deafening lament even drowned out the motorcycle noise of the comings and goings of Crenshaw's fellow bikers.

It was Santa himself who came up with the solution. The props people created a set of papier-mâché antlers, which were fitted to Luthor's head so he became an instant reindeer, just under actual size. He sat contentedly at the foot of the throne. The only complication was that his antlers sagged a little when he turned his big head to gaze worshipfully up at Santa.

Savannah glowed. "Oh, Mr. Crenshaw, I knew you loved him back."

Santa glared at her over his thick beard. "I don't love him, kid. This was the only way he'd shut his piehole."

"What a kidder." Savannah shrugged it off. "Luthor has a way of getting under people's skin."

"Yeah," Ben agreed feelingly. "Usually by sinking his fangs into it."

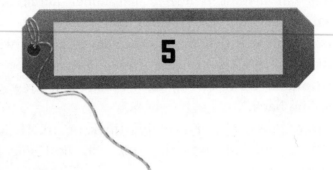

5

As the days progressed, the elves got better in spite of themselves.

The dancing improved. The singing improved. The costumes became more bearable. Or, at least, Griffin and his friends got used to the discomfort. Santa continued to be his obnoxious self, but even that was getting to be part of the routine.

"I almost prefer it this way," Griffin observed. "He doesn't bug us to be perfect elves, because he cares as much about Santa's Workshop as he cares about everything else—zero."

The Holiday Spectacular was a project of the Colchester family. But Mr. Colchester had nothing to do with it except occasionally to stick his nose into the Great Hall and declare, "Excellent! Keep up the good work!" He said the same thing regardless of whether he was walking in on Tiffany's charming solo, Mr. O'Bannon rewiring the fourth blown transformer of the day, or Luthor bumping into a ladder and sending a workman plunging to a broken ankle. It was all progress to Charles Colchester because he didn't have to worry about it.

The person who did have to worry about it was Priddle. But the secretary was so very proper and so very British that it was impossible to tell whether or not he was stressed about anything. He never smiled; then again, he never really frowned, either. His clipped accent and hundred-dollar vocabulary made it nearly impossible for the elves to figure out what it was he wanted them to do. They knew that "a bit of all right" rated higher than "a spot of bother," and being in "rather a tight corner" was very bad.

"I wish he spoke English," commented Melissa plaintively.

"Are you kidding?" crowed Logan. "All the best directors have accents."

He was making no progress at all with the one director he needed to impress—Yvette Boucle. Nor was he having any success making a friend of her daughter. Tiffany was so convinced that everything Darren said and did was hilarious and brilliant that she barely noticed Logan.

"It's so unfair!" the young actor complained. "Tiffany is a fellow performer. We have everything in common. What does she see in Darren?"

"Trust me," Griffin advised. "Any girl who's demented enough to have a crush on Vader is a good person to stay away from."

"He doesn't even care about her," Logan muttered. "All he wants to do is kiss up to Russell."

It was working, too. On Thursday, Griffin and Ben arrived at the Colchester mansion to find Darren already there, still in his pajamas, pouring himself a bowl of cereal in the pantry.

"What are you doing here, Vader?" Griffin asked irritably. "What happened to your clothes?"

"I'll probably change straight into my elf suit," Darren replied smugly. "My man Russ and I were up late watching movies, so he invited me to sleep over." He sighed wanly. "It's so nice to hang out with classy people for a change."

"You don't care about class," Griffin accused. "You just care about money. This so-called friendship is totally bogus, just like you."

"That's where you're wrong, Bing. Russ and I have an uncommon bond. He usually comes to visit his grandfather in the summer. But everybody our age is away at camp then. Now, finally, he gets to hang out with the classiest kid in town, *moi*. And I'm making myself his personal survival guide to Cedarville."

"What do you know about survival?" Ben demanded.

"Plenty. For example, if you see a guy with a weasel in his shirt, back off. You don't want to catch a case of stupid. Ditto anyone who calls himself 'The Man With The Plan.' And there's this inventor in town who dreams up some pretty moronic stuff. Like, oh, let's say Fruit Armor—"

34

Griffin saw red. "If Fruit Armor is so moronic, how come your mother is taking our money to file the patent?"

"She's not filing so fast, Bing," Darren told him confidentially. "She thinks Fruit Armor might be too dumb to be a real thing. Honest, I spoke up for your dad. I said, 'If aliens invade Earth, what's going to protect our apples from their killer death ray?'"

Griffin was close to exploding. He was used to Darren's abuse. But when the attacks extended to Mr. Bing and his inventions, it really put him over the edge. Darren only knew about them because of his mother's legal work for Mr. Bing. And besides, before an invention was patented, it had to be top secret or someone else could steal the idea.

"The chef's making me pancakes if you want some," came a voice.

A bleary-eyed Russell, also in pajamas, shuffled into the kitchen. "Oh," he added, spying Griffin and Ben. "Hi."

Griffin got right in Darren's face, glaring up into the bigger boy's eyes. "You better cut it out, Vader—"

"Hey," said Russell, his tone rising. "Step off!"

Griffin sized up Charles Colchester's spoiled grandson. Russell seemed to be ready for an argument he knew he could win. Being named Colchester made him automatically in the right.

Russell wasn't done yet. "You Cedarville types blow me away. Who do you think you are? You're stuck in this frozen wasteland—seriously, when the next ice age starts, how will anybody here even notice? And you have the *nerve* to act like you're the only people who know how to live! Where do you get off messing with *my* friend in *my* house?"

"Sorry," Ben put in quickly as Griffin choked back his anger. "This is kind of a longtime thing between Darren and us. We didn't mean to involve you in it."

"I could get you kicked out of here, you know," Russell threatened. "All it would take is one word from me!"

"Hey," Griffin retorted. "We're the ones giving up our vacation to help out with your grandfather's pageant. Please don't act like you have no clue who's doing who a favor. It's pretty obvious that you hate being an elf even more than the rest of us!"

Russell grimaced. "At least I'm not from the one-horse town where everybody thinks Santa's Workshop is like Disneyland. Ever since kindergarten, I've been fighting off Grandpa's attempts to bring me up here for the holidays. And if my parents weren't on their second honeymoon, I'd be with them somewhere—anywhere but this dump!"

Griffin turned to Darren. "Come on, Vader. You're from Cedarville, too. Are you going to stand by and let him bad-mouth our town?"

Darren grinned. "I'm a citizen of the world, Bing. Anywhere I go, that's home."

"How about Antarctica?" Ben suggested. "And stay there."

The chef entered the pantry carrying a steaming platter of pancakes and bacon. As the tray was lowered to table level, Ferret Face darted out of Ben's jerkin, snatched up a strip of bacon, and disappeared once again into the shelter of Ben's clothing. It was all over before the platter actually settled onto the tabletop.

"We can't eat that now," Russell complained. "It's contaminated!"

Darren helped himself to a stack of pancakes and reached for the syrup. "Don't worry. The weasel's clean."

Loud slurping noises came from inside Ben's shirt.

Griffin smiled broadly. "Now, that's class—Cedarville style."

6

Opening night for the Holiday Spectacular was set for December 18. Bathed in red and green floodlights, the Colchester mansion glowed like an enormous ornament placed with care on the shore of Long Island Sound. Across the large waterfront property, eight inches of fresh powder completed the winter tableau. It hadn't actually snowed yet that year, but Charles Colchester had hired snowmaking trucks from a ski resort to groom his rolling lawns. He called it "Instant White Christmas." Everything had to be perfect for his illustrious family's annual gift to Cedarville.

The start time was six p.m., but by five, people were lined up twelve deep up and down the long circular drive. There were families not just from Cedarville, but the neighboring towns, the boroughs of New York City, and as far away as New Jersey and Connecticut. Cars lined both sides of the most exclusive street in town, in defiance of the hand-lettered NO PARKING signs put up by Miss Grier. Traffic was reduced to a trickle in either direction as new arrivals searched for open spots on the shoulder.

A deafening roar shattered the night as an ancient backfiring Harley-Davidson peeled down the center line of the road, its wide handlebars threading the needle between cars by no more than an inch or two on either side. Scattering stunned spectators, the big machine accelerated up the drive and disappeared around the side of the mansion. None of them would ever have believed that the hulking black-jacketed goon riding the Harley was the same person as the jolly, rosy-cheeked, white-bearded Santa they were all standing in line to see.

Inside the mansion, Santa's elves waited nervously for the pageant to begin. The Great Hall was quiet now, but that was deceiving. Soon it would be packed to the rafters, and the crowd would include neighbors, teachers, parents, family, and friends.

There were butterflies in everybody's stomachs, but Logan's insides buzzed with a swarm of agitated bees. To him, Santa's Workshop wasn't just an annual holiday pageant. It was a *performance*, and there was nothing the young actor took more seriously than that.

He had already appeared in several commercials, but those were just thirty-second spots for toilet paper and athlete's foot cream. The next step was to land a place in a real theater company. The North Shore Players were tailor-made for Logan—local, yet close enough to New York to attract Broadway critics. From there, it would be just a short step to Hollywood!

Standing in the way of that dream was Yvette Boucle. Tonight he would deliver a performance as an elf so powerful, so nuanced, and so three-dimensional that she'd have no choice but to let him into the North Shore Players!

Priddle gave the signal to open the mansion's grand main doors. Families poured inside. Little kids ran straight for the miniature castle that housed the empty throne. Their parents hung back, surveying the North Pole scene that many of them had been visiting ever since they themselves were children. Inevitably, their eyes found the tree and traveled up its twenty-five-foot height to rest on the Star of Prague, the Holiday Spectacular's crowning glory.

Logan witnessed all this peering through a crack in the doorway to the Great Hall. The excited babble from so many young throats swelled into a single refrain:

"We want Santa! We want Santa! We want Santa!"

From beneath the red fabric of the Santa suit, a gurgle issued from Dirk Crenshaw's stomach.

"Man, that enchilada keeps coming up on me!" he announced.

Priddle slipped into the anteroom, clapping for attention. "Places, everyone. We can't keep our young fans waiting any longer. Good luck."

"You're supposed to say 'Break a leg,'" Logan piped up. Then he looked at Tiffany to make sure she noticed he knew the theatrical lingo.

"I'd prefer that you'd not use that term." Priddle sniffed tensely. "Please be careful out there."

Savannah leaned over to her beloved dog. "Okay, sweetie. It's time."

Majestically capped by his papier-mâché antlers, Luthor began to heave forward, pulling Santa's wheeled sleigh out into the Great Hall. The elves flanked him on both sides, ready to lend a hand if the big Doberman's strength faltered. It never did.

The reaction from the crowd was pure pandemonium. Little kids rushed the procession. It was all the elves could do to keep them from attacking Santa in a horde. This was a lot more like bodyguarding than acting, Logan reflected in annoyance. Then again, Tiffany would probably understand, since she was holding off three crazed kindergartners on the other side.

Luckily, it was only a short distance to the castle, and the kids fell into line once Santa took his place on the throne. Mr. Colchester made a speech declaring the Holiday Spectacular on, and describing how proud he was that his grandson, Russell, was one of the elves this year. The sight of an up-and-coming young Colchester working hard to make the pageant a success drew an enormous ovation from the crowd. Russell looked as if he wished a sinkhole would open under the mansion and swallow him away from all the Cedarville attention. Darren awarded him a mighty slap on the back, nearly knocking him into the face-painting booth.

Then it was time for the show to begin. During the elves' dance, Logan was determined to smile a little wider and kick a little higher than everybody else. But his high-stepping foot knocked off one of Melissa's ear points, which sailed through the air and landed in a vat of gingerbread batter, where it sank out of sight.

During the caroling, Logan also tried to outsing the other elves, but the organist, Yvette Boucle, kept motioning for him to quiet down. When was he ever going to knock her socks off with his talent? Certainly not during her daughter's solo, when all he could do was hum in the background.

The next thing they knew, the performances were over and the Workshop was on full force. Dirk Crenshaw might have been a world-class slob, but he was also a world-class Santa. Or at least he looked like one. The hustle and bustle in the Great Hall covered up the fact that he never asked the kids what they wanted for Christmas, never answered their questions, and never said anything besides the occasional "Ho, ho, ho!" No one could see the earbuds hidden by his bushy white beard, and the pine scent of the North Pole covered the smell of stale cigars and the garlic breath from his enchilada dinner.

The elves were in charge of directing traffic in and out of the throne room. The job was easier than Logan had expected, due to the presence of Luthor. Antlers or not, a guard dog was still a guard dog. Santa may have been making a list and checking it twice, but he would never tear you to pieces. You couldn't say the same thing about his reindeer. It kept the line moving.

The whole town was there, drinking mulled cider, decorating gingerbread men, and visiting the various booths, playing games, and having a wonderful time. Cedarville Middle School was well represented, and the elves took some good-natured ribbing about their costumes. This was balanced by their parents, who were glowing with pride.

Also glowing was Mr. Colchester, who mingled with the crowd, shaking hands and accepting congratulations on yet another successful Holiday Spectacular. Even sour-faced Priddle seemed thrilled with the evening. Every few minutes he would pass through the castle with a new statistic: "We've broken the all-time attendance record for opening night" or "We've sold all the tickets for the charity raffle" or "Which one of you comedians dropped an elf ear into the cookie batter?" For this last comment, he held up a freshly baked gingerbread man with what looked like a shark fin growing out of its back.

The night was magical. Excited shouts rang out as kids ran from the bouncy castle to the gingerbread house to the fishpond to Santa's throne room. The cluster of booths resembled a Bavarian village, and the Great Hall's wall sconces were festooned with pine boughs and red satin bows. The tree was the glittering focal point of it all, dripping with tinsel and hung with magnificent ornaments. And at the summit, the most magnificent of them all.

The festivities went on. No one wanted to be the first to leave.

It might have continued long past the ten o'clock closing. But at exactly 8:57, Santa's Workshop was plunged into sudden darkness.

7

The lively holiday background music stopped abruptly. All sounds of electronics and machinery ceased. Inside the thick walls of the Colchester mansion, the blackness was suffocating, falling over everything like a dense velvet cloth. It would have been scary under the best of circumstances. With so many people crowded together in an unfamiliar place, it was nothing short of terrifying.

Children wailed in fear. Parents called for their kids. Everyone began moving at the same time, bumping, tripping, and running into one another. What had been a charming Bavarian village mere seconds ago was now an impossible obstacle course that everyone had to navigate blind.

"Remain calm!" the not-at-all-calm voice of Charles Colchester rang out in the midst of the void. "There's no cause for panic!"

His guests did not agree. As frightened families

struggled to find each other in the dark, the wipeouts and collisions grew more common and more spectacular.

"Mr. O'Bannon!" Priddle called stridently.

"It's a power failure!" came the electrician's reply over the chaos.

"I can see that," Priddle persisted. "My question is, can you fix it?"

"Fix it? I can't even find it! I can't see my hand in front of my face!"

By this time, several phone flashlights were illuminated, which provided a glow for people to make their way to the mansion's double doors. It wasn't much brighter out there, since the power failure extended over the whole property. But at least there was space for the Workshop escapees to spread out. There they milled, getting their feet wet in the artificially generated snow.

"Wouldn't you know it?" Ben complained. "They bring in a machine to make fake snow and I end up soaking in it in elf slippers." He shifted from leg to leg, which made the bells jingle.

"This is no time to worry about wet feet!" Savannah rushed over. "Where's Luthor?"

"Where do you think?" Griffin gestured toward the crowd on the far side of the birdbath. "With his new best friend."

The Doberman, his antlers slightly askew, had just emerged from the mansion and now stood with Dirk Crenshaw. The hulking biker was navigating the darkness by the glowing tip of a humongous cigar.

"It figures," Pitch commented. "Santa Clod and his faithful reindeer."

Savannah watched them. "Mr. Crenshaw must be a really wonderful person if Luthor feels such a strong connection."

A cloud of cigar smoke wafted over in their direction. It made Ferret Face cough.

"That's not the only strong thing about him," Ben observed.

Logan came staggering out of the mansion, latched on to Tiffany with one hand and her mother with the other.

"We're fine!" Mrs. Boucle kept insisting in annoyance.

Logan's friends recognized the expression on his face all too well. The young actor had finally found a dramatic moment, and he was milking it for all it was worth.

"Don't worry about me!" he emoted. "The important thing is you're safe!"

"We're *all* safe," Tiffany told him. "You are, too, in case you haven't noticed."

"You don't have to thank me," Logan insisted. "True courage is its own reward."

Darren was next out the door, ready with a wise-crack, as usual. "Relax, Kellerman." He snorted. "It's a power failure, not an air raid."

A peal of laughter escaped Tiffany. "You're so funny!" she gushed at him.

Eventually, the Great Hall emptied completely, and families gathered together on the grounds.

"Well, this was a pretty memorable Santa's Workshop," Mr. Bing put in drily.

Mrs. Slovak was upset. "I've been coming here since I was a little girl, and I can't recall an incident like this."

"Mr. O'Bannon was worried something might happen," her son told her. "All week he's been warning that the old wiring can't take the kind of overload we're putting on it."

"Hey, where's Melissa?" Pitch asked Mr. Dukakis.

"Oh, she stayed inside the mansion to help Mr. O'Bannon," Melissa's father replied.

"That's good," Griffin approved. "She could rewire the whole house with both hands tied behind her back." The shy girl's expertise with computers and technology was legendary in Cedarville.

As if on cue, the lights blazed on in the mansion. A big cheer went up on the snowy lawn. The crowd surged back in through the double doors, eager for more holiday fun.

All at once, a scream of agony was heard in the Great Hall. Griffin and the elves pushed their way to the front. There stood their host and patron, Charles Colchester, his normally ruddy face drained of all color.

Santa's Workshop was a shambles—booths and tables knocked over, drinks and trampled snacks scattered across the floor, blobs of spilled gingerbread dough smeared everywhere, the bouncy castle flat as a pancake, Santa's throne lying broken on its side.

Yet it was not the damage that had devastated Cedarville's most prominent citizen. Griffin followed the man's horrified gaze to the top of the soaring Christmas tree.

The Star of Prague was gone.

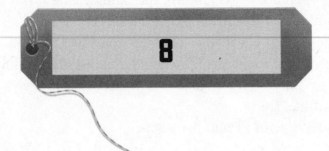

8

The scene on TV was instantly familiar to Griffin—the Colchester mansion lit up like a picture postcard, its rolling lawns covered in a blanket of white snow. But the hundreds of cars that had been wedged into every available parking space around the gracious old home last night had been replaced by only three—police cars, their flashers lighting up the night.

"... *Electric company officials estimate that the blackout lasted between twelve and fifteen minutes,*" came the news anchor's voice, "*and affected only the mansion where the Holiday Spectacular was being held. During that time, the thieves must have removed the antique Czech masterpiece from the top of the tree and spirited it away in the darkness and confusion. So far, Cedarville police have been unable to confirm any reports of a vehicle leaving the area at around that time. This gives rise to an alternate theory of the crime in which the Star of Prague was hidden somewhere in or around the Colchester home to be picked up later. This seems unlikely, however, as a thorough search of the premises has turned up nothing."*

"What a horrible thing to happen!" Mrs. Bing exclaimed. "I feel so bad for the Colchesters— especially after all they've done for Cedarville."

"I know," Griffin agreed. Yet he couldn't help but enjoy a little relief. Here he was, sprawled out on the couch in the comfort of a T-shirt and sweatpants, instead of crammed into his elf costume, humiliating himself in front of a crowd of hundreds. It was a selfish and not-very-nice way to feel, but he felt it all the same.

"Art historians have traced the Star of Prague all the way back to the tenth century," the news anchor went on. *"It was commissioned by Wenceslaus the First, Duke of Bohemia, the subject of the popular Christmas carol 'Good King Wenceslas.' For this reason, it has been estimated that the Star might fetch as much as ten million dollars at auction. It has been the property of the Colchester family for eight generations. While occasionally loaned out to museums from Tulsa to Timbuktu, the masterpiece has always been back in its place of honor atop the tree in the Great Hall for the Colchesters' annual Holiday Spectacular. Until today."*

At this point, the screen cut to a shot of Charles Colchester. He looked decades older than the man Griffin had seen during elf rehearsal at the mansion. His eyes were red-rimmed and puffy, as if he hadn't slept since the theft of his Star.

"Our family has been holding the Santa's Workshop Holiday Spectacular since before I was born. I attended as a young boy, and this year I welcomed my grandson to Long Island so that he could experience the tradition he would one day pass on to his own children. I never thought of it as our gift to the town; it was something we shared as neighbors and friends. But the idea that someone in Cedarville would turn our generosity against us—" The great man's voice became shaky. *"Well, I see now what a fool I was to believe we were part of this community."*

At this point, he turned away from the microphone, overcome with emotion. Mr. and Mrs. Bing were filled with sympathy and regret as the broadcast cut back to the news anchor at her desk.

"This year's pageant has been canceled and all future Holiday Spectaculars have been put on hold. A spokesman for the Colchester family said they're considering leaving Cedarville for good."

"Leaving?" Mrs. Bing sat forward in alarm. "The Colchesters have been here for a hundred and fifty years! It wouldn't be Cedarville without them!"

Griffin's father shrugged unhappily. "I guess when the Star got stolen, Charles took it personally. Almost like the entire town had stabbed his family in the back."

"That's ridiculous!" his wife retorted. "I'm sure no one from *Cedarville* took the Star of Prague."

The doorbell rang and Griffin got up to answer it,

expecting to see Ben or another one of their friends. No one was happy about last night's disaster ... but that didn't change the fact that they now had an entire two-week school break they would no longer be spending in elf mode. After all, sitting around being miserable wouldn't bring back the stolen masterpiece.

He opened the door to find himself looking up at a tall uniformed policeman with dark eyes under heavy brows. "Long time no see, Griffin. Miss me?"

Griffin's parents were on their feet. "Detective Sergeant Vizzini!" blurted Mrs. Bing. "What are you doing here?"

"Nice to see you folks, too." The officer stepped past Griffin into the house. He looked around the living room. "New wallpaper, huh? I like the color."

This was not Vizzini's first visit to the Bing home. Nor was it the second or even the third. Cedarville had a small police department, and Griffin's schemes had attracted their attention several times in the past. It had always worked out in the end. The Man With The Plan was usually found to be innocent or at least well meaning. Still, it was pretty unnerving when the big cop came calling.

"Exactly what can we do for you, Detective?" asked Mr. Bing.

Vizzini nodded in the direction of the TV, which was still tuned to coverage of the Colchester story. "I see you're up to speed on the theft of the Star of Prague. I understand Griffin was on the scene last night."

"We all were," Mrs. Bing supplied. "Griffin happens to be an elf in this year's Holiday Spectacular. I mean, he *was* an elf before the pageant was canceled."

The officer turned his attention on Griffin. "And what were you doing at the moment the Star disappeared?"

"Wait a minute," Mr. Bing interjected sharply. "Surely you're not accusing *Griffin*?"

"I'm just gathering information," Vizzini assured them. "Something valuable has gone missing. That's happened a few times before around here—a rare baseball card, a winning lottery ticket, a Super Bowl ring. Put yourself in my shoes. Where would you start to look? Your son has always been tangled up in it somehow."

"It's okay, Dad. I've got nothing to hide." Griffin faced the policeman. "I was in the throne room putting kids on Santa's lap when the power failure happened."

"And then?"

"You couldn't really move in the dark," Griffin replied. "It was too crowded. People were bumping into things and each other. The little kids were crying; parents were calling out names; everybody was pushing and shoving. So I just stayed put until Mr. Priddle told us to evacuate. Then you could kind of follow the crowd almost like you were riding a wave. I stayed in the yard until the lights came back on."

During this explanation, Vizzini took out a ring-bound pad and began writing furiously. The scratching sound of his pen was like fingernails against a black-board to Griffin. In his experience, the trouble usually started when Vizzini made notes.

At last, the dark eyes looked up from the pad. "And do you have any witnesses who can back up your story?"

"Well, uh, Pitch was with me—"

"You mean Antonia Benson, who could use her climbing skills to scale the tree to reach the Star of Prague?" Vizzini jumped in, flipping through his notes.

"Uh, yeah. Also Logan—"

"Logan Kellerman, your frequent accomplice, who submitted your name for the Holiday Spectacular in the first place?"

Griffin frowned. "Plus Savannah was there—"

"The Drysdale girl whose dog played a reindeer in the pageant and could easily have been trained to create a distraction?"

"And Ben—"

"Your best friend, whose small size would enable him to move through a crowd in the dark without being noticed," the policeman concluded.

Griffin's frown deepened to a grimace.

The big cop spoke again. "You left out Melissa Dukakis, whose expertise with electronics would make it child's play for her to manufacture a power failure."

"Actually, Melissa wasn't with us the whole time," Griffin told him. "She stayed inside to help the electrician fix the faulty wiring."

No sooner had the words passed his lips than he wished he'd kept his mouth shut. That made it sound even worse. The note-making pen was just a blur.

All the things Vizzini was saying were true, but the detective seemed to be painting a picture to show that Griffin and his friends had volunteered to be elves just so they could get their hands on the Star of Prague!

Come to think of it, that was exactly how Griffin's plans usually worked—he assembled a team of kids with special abilities and devised a way to combine those talents to achieve a goal. If they had wanted to heist the Star, the dark-eyed officer had just described the perfect operation to get it done.

Oh, man, Detective Sergeant Vizzini knows me better than I know myself!

There was only one thing wrong with what Vizzini was saying: Griffin was innocent. They all were.

Mr. Bing spoke up again. "I know Griffin and his friends have a bit of a . . . track record—"

"We call it *a pattern of behavior,*" the cop interrupted.

"But this isn't even realistic," Griffin's father argued. "A baseball card is tiny. The Star of Prague is bigger than a basketball, solid glass, heavy and fragile. You've got to be joking if you think middle schoolers took it right under the noses of, like, four hundred people."

"We don't do joking in law enforcement," Vizzini informed him solemnly. "Comedy isn't a core subject at the police academy. We like facts. The Star of Prague is missing. That's a fact, because otherwise it would still be at the top of that tree. And I'm talking to your son because he and his friends have been involved in this kind of thing before. Another fact." He flipped his notebook shut and put it away in his jacket pocket. "I think we're done here. Thanks for your time." To Griffin he added, "I hope we won't be seeing more of each other this holiday."

As soon as the officer had left, Griffin found himself locked in the crossbeams of his parents' twin glares.

"What?" He raised his hands in a gesture of innocence. "You just told Vizzini you believed me."

"*Should* we believe you?" his mother probed.

"Of course! What would I want with a thousand-year-old stained-glass star?"

Dad made a sour face. "You'll excuse us for thinking of you whenever we hear things like 'ten million dollars.'"

"Those other times weren't about the *money*," Griffin said sincerely. "They were about justice and doing the right thing, even if it didn't always work out that way. But the Star of Prague means nothing to me. I honestly never thought twice about it till it disappeared."

Mrs. Bing put an arm around her son's shoulders. "All right. We won't panic, then. The police are probably just as upset as everybody else and that's why they're jumping to conclusions. The whole community is devastated about what happened to the Colchesters. And it just won't be Christmas without Santa's Workshop. Estelle Slovak had an idea. She thinks we should all step up our own holiday displays. Get some spirit back in Cedarville."

Mr. Bing nodded. "We've been leaning on the Colchesters for too long. Nobody around here remembers how to celebrate because we're used to one family doing all the heavy lifting. That ends today. Have we still got that extra box of lights in the basement?"

"A box of lights won't help me with the police," Griffin mourned. "That guy barely stopped short of arresting me and my friends for stealing the Star."

"Detective Vizzini was just overreacting because the news is so fresh and raw," his mother soothed. "When the shock wears off, he'll see that it couldn't possibly have been you. And maybe lights *will* help a little. Everybody will calm down once they see that the holidays aren't totally ruined because of one bad thing."

Griffin ran his mind over the meeting with the tall policeman. He had seen that expression on Vizzini's face before—bland and unemotional, yet absolutely relentless. A predator that would follow its prey to the ends of the earth.

Those were not good memories for Griffin.

He and his friends had to protect themselves—and there was only one surefire way to accomplish that.

It was time for a plan.

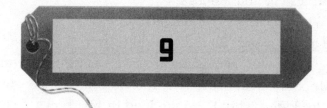

9

The reindeer stood like a column of soldiers in Ben's front hall, leaning against the wall.

Luthor sidled up to the one nearest the door, adjusting his posture so that it mirrored the plastic decoration. Except for the antlers, the big Doberman was a perfect size match. The comparison seemed to confuse him. *He* had once worn antlers similar to these, but that didn't happen anymore. What had changed? His canine brain couldn't quite make sense of it all.

Ferret Face poked his head out of Ben's shirt, watching the dog.

"Don't even think about it, pal," Ben warned the little creature. "There's no such thing as a Christmas ferret."

Savannah was there, too, but she only had eyes for the Doberman. "Poor Luthor's been moping around ever since the Holiday Spectacular got canceled. He really misses Dirk."

There was a knock at the door and Ben admitted Logan, Pitch, and Melissa.

"Where's Griffin?" Pitch asked.

"On his way," Ben promised. "Over the phone, he said it was really important that we meet this morning."

Mr. Slovak appeared at the bottom of the stairs. "Oh, hi, kids—whoa!" He stopped in his tracks. "That's a lot of reindeer."

"It isn't even all of them," Ben informed him. "Dasher's leg broke off, Blitzen won't light up, and there's a short circuit in Rudolph's nose."

His father looked exhausted. "I just spent three hours blowing up the inflatable snowman."

"All our folks are doing it, Mr. Slovak," Logan explained. "Everybody's trying to get into the spirit of the season since the Holiday Spectacular got shut down."

Mr. Slovak's gaze traveled the length of the reindeer team to its payload—a huge sleigh bearing a smiling, red-suited Saint Nick. Then he turned to the menorah on the table at the base of the stairs. It seemed alone and forlorn. "Seems a little one-sided," he said finally. "I mean, we're Jewish, too."

Melissa agitated her head to part her curtain of hair. "The point is to show holiday spirit," she said seriously. "I don't think it matters which holiday you're showing spirit for."

"I guess I always figured it would be a little more . . . evenhanded," Mr. Slovak reasoned.

"But there are tons of Christmas decorations you can buy," Ben told his father. "Hanukkah's great, but it just doesn't have as much stuff. You can't deck the halls with menorahs. Most people only have one."

In answer, Mr. Slovak pulled his coat off the rack and shrugged into it. "If your mother asks, I'm at the mall. I might be a while." He opened the door and brushed past Griffin, who was coming up the walk. "Hi, Griffin. Bye, Griffin." He got into his car and sped off.

"What's up with your dad?" Griffin asked Ben.

"Not a big reindeer fan," Ben replied. "What's so urgent that we had to drop everything and meet?"

"Guys," said Griffin, "Detective Sergeant Vizzini was at my house yesterday."

"That's old news," Pitch informed him. "He was at my house, too. At this point, my folks just yawn and put on a pot of coffee when they see the squad car in our driveway."

One by one, the others confirmed that they, too, had been visited by the tall policeman.

"Don't you think it's a problem that the cops suspect us of stealing the Star of Prague?" Griffin challenged.

"This is called 'being innocent,'" Ben lectured. "It's unfamiliar to you because we're usually guilty up to our necks. But in the end, who cares what Vizzini suspects? We didn't do it. He can search all our houses from top to bottom and he won't find the Star."

"It doesn't matter that we're innocent if everybody

thinks we're guilty," Griffin argued. "Vizzini will never leave us alone—the guy's like a horsefly who's after a taste of your blood. And it's not just him. My mom called for a hair appointment and got a long lecture about how her son's greed had ruined the holidays for everybody else. Then they made her wait on hold for twenty minutes before connecting her to the fax machine."

Pitch raised an eyebrow. "You know, that kind of explains what happened to us last night. My dad took us out to this fancy dinner. You know, to make up for no climbing trip—like that could ever happen. Anyway, when they saw us, they tried to pretend we didn't have a reservation. Finally, they gave us the worst table in the place, right next to the bathroom. And the whole time, the waiters and busboys were shooting me these dirty looks."

"My mom picked up our clothes from the cleaners and mine were all blue," Logan announced.

"That could be an accident," Ben suggested.

"Just *my* stuff—nobody else's?" Logan insisted. "The cleaners have little kids—big Santa's Workshop fans."

"You see?" Griffin was triumphant. "And it's only going to get worse as the rumors spread about whose fault it is that the holidays stink."

"Is that why you called us here?" Pitch growled. "To explain why our names are mud in this town?"

"Our names are mud *now*," Griffin amended. "They don't have to stay that way—*if* we take action."

62

From his back pocket, he produced a sheet of paper. The others watched as he unfolded it in front of them. Even Luthor, who had been moping around in front of the plastic Santa, looked on in interest. Ferret Face peered down from Ben's collar.

OPERATION STARCHASER

"Operation?" Ben blurted. "But that's a—"

"A plan," finished Pitch, her expression severe. "Griffin, you know we don't do the p-word anymore—not unless it's an emergency. How many times did we almost get ourselves thrown in jail? How many times did our parents threaten to string us up by our thumbs? And it's even more dangerous now that Vizzini is nosing around."

"That's why Operation Starchaser is so important," Griffin reasoned. "We have to figure out who stole the Star of Prague just to prove that it wasn't us. Think about it: If the Colchesters leave Cedarville, we'll never be off the hook. How'd you like to spend the rest of your life as the town Scrooge?"

"Worse than Scrooge," mused Logan. "He was a cheapskate and a jerk, but at least he never stole anything."

"Exactly." Griffin held up the paper for the others to read:

OPERATION STARCHASER

GOALS:
Solve the MYSTERY of the missing STAR OF PRAGUE.
Get it back to the COLCHESTERS.

SUSPECT LIST:

DIRK "FINGERS" CRENSHAW—Sleazeball Santa
Motive: Needs CASH to pay off GAMBLING DEBTS.
Why would an unfriendly, knuckle-dragging biker get a job
as a Santa if he wasn't up to something?

MR. O'BANNON—Overstressed Electrician
Motive: Doesn't want to NURSEMAID the mansion's
old wiring through another Holiday Spectacular and get
blamed when it goes APEWIRE.
Who better to fake a power failure than an electrician?

MISS GRIER—Disgruntled Neighbor.
Motive: To END the TRAFFIC and NOISE caused by
Santa's Workshop.
She's been crabbing about the Holiday Spectacular for fifty
years.

YVETTE BOUCLE—Rebuffed Researcher
Motive: Needs ACCESS to the Star for the BOOK she's
writing.

If the Colchesters won't let her get close to the Star, why not steal it right out from under their noses? The crime will only make the subject of her book even more famous.

MR. PRIDDLE—Fed-up Flunky
Motive: To put a STOP to the Holiday Spectacular ONCE AND FOR ALL.
Most of the work falls on him. Therefore nobody benefits more if the Holiday Spectacular goes away.

DARREN VADER—Money-grubbing Meathead
Motive: Sheer GREED.
The guy would sell his own mother for fifty cents, so imagine what he'd do for a ten-million-dollar glass ornament.

Pitch was dubious. "As much as I hate to say it, I'm pretty sure Vader's innocent. How does ripping off the kid's grandfather help him suck up to Russell?"

"Plus he was out of the house just a few minutes after we were," Ben added. "It's not like you can hide the Star under an elf suit—not even *his* size."

"Not unless he stashed it somewhere as soon as he stole it," mused Melissa.

Logan shook his head. "But didn't Vizzini say the cops searched the Colchester mansion? Surely they would have found it."

"I'm not saying it's definitely Vader," Griffin reminded them. "A lot of the suspects were on the lawn with us.

How come it took them so long to get there? We had to fight the same crowd, work our way through the same obstacle course. If you think about it, we should have been last out, since we started inside the throne room."

"Well, there's no way Dirk did it," Savannah put in positively. "Luthor could never love a felon." She indicated the Doberman, who was rubbing up against Santa's sleigh, whining mournfully.

"Mrs. Boucle didn't steal anything, either," added Logan. "The theater attracts only high-quality people."

"Which is why there are six suspects," Griffin explained. "Five of them have to be innocent. Operation Starchaser is going to help us figure out who isn't."

Pitch folded her arms in front of her. "And that happens how?"

With a flourish, Griffin flipped the paper over to the reverse side.

STEP 1: Surveillance . . . .

There was an audible groan. Nothing was more boring than skulking around in people's bushes, waiting for evidence or a clue that might never come.

"Come on, you guys, maybe it won't be so bad," Griffin offered. "A ten-million-dollar art treasure can't be the easiest thing to hide—especially if you're trying to sell it. Find the Star and we've found our thief."

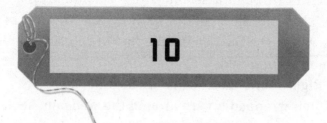

10

Thirty feet off the ground, Pitch appeared to be the size of a squirrel. She certainly scrambled up the trunk of the tree with the ease of one. For a member of the Benson family, climbing was as natural as breathing.

From below, Griffin and Ben watched her crawl out onto a sturdy limb that extended toward the wall of the Colchester mansion. From her jacket pocket, she produced a small object and placed it on the branch. Then she spoke into a miniature walkie-talkie clipped to the collar of her coat.

"How's that?" her voice crackled through the unit in Griffin's hand.

"Melissa?" Griffin asked.

Melissa was listening through another walkie-talkie. She was at home in her room, which served as tech headquarters for Operation Starchaser. "Tilt it just a little to the left."

Pitch manipulated the tiny webcam, and the video

feed on Melissa's laptop came into perfect focus. It peered in through a second-story window of the mansion, showing the upstairs hallway and the top of the tree, where the Star of Prague had once gleamed in all its multicolored glory.

"Right there," Melissa confirmed.

Pitch wrapped a wire around the webcam, securing it into place on the branch. Then she descended to place another, where it would keep watch over the service entrance to the mansion—the one that the elves had used.

"I'll never get used to the way she flits around up there," Ben commented nervously. "What would we do if she fell?"

"Pitch doesn't fall," Griffin said confidently. "That tree will hit the ground before she does."

She was halfway back down to ground level when Melissa's urgent warning came through the walkie-talkie.

"Freeze!"

Her voice was so emphatic that Ferret Face clutched at Ben's chest with all four paws.

"Ow!"

"What is it?" Griffin asked in a low voice.

"Someone's coming out of the house," she hissed.

Griffin grabbed Ben by the wrist and the two ducked into the shelter of a toolshed. As he slid the doors silently shut, he caught a glimpse of Priddle, his three-piece suit immaculate, stepping out onto the walkway. Twenty feet above them, Pitch plastered herself around the far side of the tree trunk, out of Priddle's view.

Crouched amid the gardening tools, Ben turned terrified eyes on his best friend. Griffin put a hand over Ben's mouth. "Not a sound," he whispered. To be caught on the Colchester property so soon after the theft of the Star would look very, very bad.

But the voice they heard next was not Priddle's aristocratic English accent.

"I've been afraid of something like this for years," Mr. O'Bannon, the electrician, lamented from outside the shed. "See? The melting snow seeped through this crack in the foundation. There's an electrical box in the cellar just below there. It shorted out the wires, and poof!"

"Melting snow." The personal assistant sighed. "In a year when we haven't seen so much as a flake. But that's not festive enough for Charles Colchester. He has to groom the entire property like a ski slope."

"I feel bad for the boss," Mr. O'Bannon told him, "but I can't say I'm sorry to see the end of Santa's Workshop. Keeping the power flowing to all those lights and machines is a hassle I don't need. I always knew something like this might happen. But I never dreamed somebody would be low enough to use it to steal the Star of Prague."

"The human animal is a complex creature," Priddle agreed philosophically. "But this black cloud may indeed have a silver lining. I've never seen Mr. Colchester so disillusioned and upset. I suspect we both have suffered through our last Holiday Spectacular. A lost art treasure is a small price to pay for that."

The electrician sounded surprised. "I know why *I've* got a problem with Santa's Workshop. But what's your beef with it?"

"The reason I chose not to have children of my own is because I abhor them," Priddle replied honestly. "The Holiday Spectacular is a seasonally recurring nightmare I'll have no difficulty living without."

Griffin turned to Ben and mouthed the words: *He hates kids*. That was extra motive to throw a monkey wrench into Santa's Workshop.

Priddle spoke again. "Strange. I could have sworn these doors had been closed all the way."

Griffin and Ben dove under a tarpaulin, cracking their heads together as they sought cover in the company of a small lawn tractor. Priddle shut the doors, blotting out what little light was in the shed.

The boys cowered there, barely daring to breathe. Griffin felt a clammy wetness soaking through the leg of his jeans. He looked down to see he was kneeling in a small puddle trickling from the end of a coil of hose. He began to shiver uncontrollably. It was *freezing*! He had to get into dry clothes before he wound up with frostbite! But how could he do that with Priddle and O'Bannon standing right there?

Fighting to control his trembling body, he got to his feet and peered out of the tarpaulin.

The scraping of the sliding doors dropped him back to the misery of the puddle. He and Ben felt, rather than heard, the footsteps of someone entering the shed. Their eyes met in agony. Who was it? Priddle? O'Bannon? Both?

"Boo!"

Both boys jumped. The sudden movement sent the tarpaulin billowing off the tractor, exposing their pink and guilty faces.

They gawked. Pitch stood in the middle of the shed, laughing at them. "You look like you've seen the zombie apocalypse!"

"Hide!" Griffin breathed.

"We're good," Pitch assured them airily. "Those guys went inside. The coast is clear."

Ben pushed an agitated Ferret Face back under his collar and glared at Pitch resentfully. "You're a real comedian."

"I know, right? Nice wet spot," she added, noting the dark shape on Griffin's pant leg.

"Leaky hose," Griffin explained, teeth chattering. "I'm g-g-glad my hypothermia is so enter-t-t-taining to you."

"Is everything okay?" Melissa's voice was so soft that the others barely heard her through the walkie-talkie.

Griffin brought up his own handset. "Let's just

71

p-p-plant the rest of the webcams and get out of here. We should probably stick a few around Miss G-G-Grier's house, too."

In spite of everything, it felt good to have a plan in action. He wondered how Logan and Savannah were doing with their parts of Operation Starchaser.

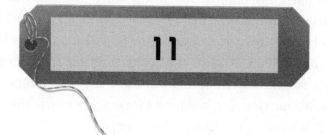

Hurry up, Mom. I want to catch them before they go out for the day."

Mrs. Kellerman made a left turn and peered across the front seat at her son. "I hope you're not still bugging Mrs. Boucle, Logan. If she doesn't need you for the North Shore Players, you have to accept that. It's her theater company, not yours."

"I'm not bugging her," Logan promised. "It isn't even her I'm going to see. I'm visiting her daughter, Tiffany."

Mrs. Kellerman was suspicious. "How do you know Yvette Boucle's daughter?"

"We were *elves* together, Mom. That's a special bonding experience. You're not in the theater, so you wouldn't understand. But when you *act* with someone, working side by side, molding your individual talents and abilities together to achieve a common creative goal, that's huge! You're like brothers—or, in Tiffany's case, sisters. I mean, I'm the brother; she's the sister."

When Griffin had been handing out the surveillance assignments for Operation Starchaser, Logan had readily volunteered to cover Yvette Boucle. It would be a no-brainer for the young actor to fall into the role of Tiffany's friend. And in the process, if he happened to really impress her mother and get her to change her mind about the North Shore Players, so much the better. It would be a win-win for everyone.

His mother sighed behind the wheel. "I hope you know what you're doing."

Logan said nothing. For theater people, knowing what you were doing was highly overrated. A true actor went with his gut. And Logan's gut was pointing in the direction of the Boucle house in Green Hollow. Only—

"*Hit the brakes!*" Logan bellowed.

Mrs. Kellerman pulled over so suddenly that the front wheels of the car bumped up over the curb. "Logan, have you lost your mind?"

Logan stared at the petite figure on the walk of a large house set well back from the road. That was Tiffany! What was she doing in Cedarville?

All at once, he recognized the stately brick home. It was the Vaders' place! Tiffany was visiting Darren. He experienced a surge of consternation. Logan would never understand what Tiffany—a fellow performer— would want with the likes of Darren.

He opened the door. "Change of plans. I'm getting out here."

"But what about Tiffany?"

"She's already here. I forgot. It's, like, an . . . elves reunion." He was babbling a little, so the line didn't ring as true as Logan might have liked. But he covered it up by scrambling out to the sidewalk and slamming the door behind him. No way was he going to let Darren steal his chance to make friends with Tiffany and impress Yvette Boucle. Logan was going to crash this little party.

It wasn't really part of his assignment. But come to think of it, Darren was a suspect, too, so this would be good for Operation Starchaser. Griffin would be pleased.

Logan called out to Tiffany, but she was already stepping inside the big house. He hurried up the long walk and rapped smartly on the door.

It took a long time for Mrs. Vader to answer. She had just admitted Tiffany and wasn't expecting another visitor so soon.

"Oh, hello. Logan, isn't it?"

Logan nodded. "I'm here to see—Darren." He almost choked on the name.

"Darren!" she called upstairs. "Your friend Logan is here!"

"Logan?" came the reply. "I don't have any friend named Logan. I know an idiot named Logan, but even he would have the brains to figure out that he's not welcome at my house."

"He's just being silly." Mrs. Vader beamed. "Go on up."

In addition to Darren and Tiffany, Logan was surprised to find Russell Colchester in the spacious bedroom. Apparently, the bromance between the rich kid and the richer kid was still on even though the Holiday Spectacular was off.

"What are you doing here, Kellerman?" Darren drawled. "Shouldn't you be home polishing your Academy Awards?"

Tiffany giggled. Even though it was meant as an insult, Logan was secretly pleased. Any reminder of Logan's acting was something she might take home to her mother.

"It sure is boring now that we're not elves anymore," Logan announced, bringing up the only thing all four of them had in common. "Russell, I figured you'd be heading back to California now that the Holiday Spectacular has been canceled."

"I wish!" Russell exclaimed fervently. "If my folks weren't in the Galápagos Islands, you wouldn't see me for dust. My grandfather's driving me nuts. You'd think the whole world ground to a halt because his stupid Star went missing."

"Yeah, what a crab," Darren added. "He's got insurance, right? Think of all the zeros *that* check is going to have!"

"Well, it's not just the money," Tiffany put in. "After all, you can't go to Walmart and pick up a new Star of Prague. My mom says it's one of the earliest examples of stained glass not built into a castle or cathedral."

Darren yawned. "And I should care about this because . . . ?"

Instead of being insulted, Tiffany laughed again.

"I'll be out of here soon," Russell went on as if no one else had spoken. "The minute my parents' plane lands at LAX, I'll be on the next flight west. Christmas should be spent on the beach, not freezing your butt off."

"But we'll be friends forever, right, Russ?" Darren held out his fist.

Russell bumped it. "You bet, man. You saved my life in this little dump of a town. Friends forever."

"Darren," Tiffany spoke up. "My mother's theater group is having their holiday party on the twenty-second and I'm allowed to bring a guest. Want to go with me?"

"No can do," Darren replied readily. "Full schedule."

"*I*'m free that night," Logan volunteered eagerly. What a golden opportunity to schmooze not just with Tiffany and her mother, but with the entire cast and crew of the North Shore Players! And, obviously, to keep an eye on Mrs. Boucle for Operation Starchaser.

"Yeah, about that," Tiffany said uncomfortably. "No offense, but my mother kind of told me to stay away from you."

"That would still be okay," Logan insisted. "I could go to the party, and you could stay away from me there."

Darren brayed a laugh. "Good one, Kellerman. Way to look desperate."

Russell seemed confused. "Are you for real?" he asked Logan.

"I'm an actor," Logan replied readily. "Being real is my business. And business is booming."

"Here's an idea," Darren suggested. "Go boom someplace else."

Naturally, Tiffany thought that was hilarious.

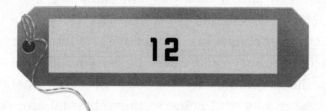

12

Luthor recognized the motorcycle right away and began to bark excitedly, craning his neck as he looked around for its owner.

It took all of Savannah's strength to pull on his leash and drag him out of the open to their hiding place around the side of the shabby apartment building. "Quiet, sweetie," she admonished. "The whole point of a stakeout is nobody's supposed to know you're there."

She reflected that maybe it wasn't such a great idea to bring her dog on this mission. His affection for the former Santa made it impossible for Luthor to control himself. It was one of the most wonderful things about the Doberman—he had so much love in his heart.

Yet already Luthor had proved valuable. Look at how quickly he had detected Crenshaw's scent on the old motorcycle—even when it was mixed with other smells, like gasoline and burnt oil.

Of course, Savannah truly believed there was no

way Dirk Crenshaw could be guilty of stealing the Star. Her faith in Luthor as a judge of character was absolute. Honestly, she had never seen the Doberman take to a stranger so quickly. A sensitive and intelligent animal like Luthor could never be so wrong. That was why she'd volunteered for this part of Operation Starchaser. She was going to prove beyond any doubt that Dirk was innocent. And then Luthor and the former Santa were going to share a joyful reunion.

They had gotten the address from Melissa, who had hacked into the e-mail accounts of the six suspects. Savannah smiled. No place in cyberspace was safe from the shy tech whiz.

According to Melissa, Dirk Crenshaw barely used e-mail at all. He seemed to believe in face-to-face communication. That would explain all the debt collectors who showed up at the Colchester mansion to hassle him about the money he owed. Maybe that was why he lived in such a crummy apartment. The Royal Flamingo Suites were not in the nicest part of Cedarville. In fact, they were right by the railroad tracks, so the clatter and roar of commuter trains went on day and night. The building reminded her of a motel her family had been forced to stay in a long time ago when every other room in five counties had been booked. Mom had bought a bottle of bleach and scrubbed down the entire place, and when Savannah and her dad had tried to use the ice machine, a sickly green liquid had dribbled out that reminded her of chilled pea soup.

Living in a bad place doesn't make you a bad person, Savannah reminded herself.

At that moment, the screen door was kicked violently open, and a cloud of smoke wafted outside. Crenshaw stepped into the swirling haze, puffing on the stub of a cigar.

Savannah's animal radar sensed that Luthor was coiled like a spring beside her, about to pounce. It would take all her dog-whispering skills to keep him from giving away their presence. She locked her arms around the Doberman's muscular neck, leaned in close to his ear, and murmured, "Shhh, sweetie. I know you want to say hello to your friend—and you will. But not just yet. Stay, Luthor. I'm right here."

She felt her dog tense up in her arms. But he did not move or bark.

Crenshaw started up the walk. He paused in front of his parked motorcycle, took a final pull of his cigar, and flicked the butt onto the driveway.

Adding littering to the long list of character traits that make him gross, Savannah concluded. But, she reminded herself, Luthor loved him, and that meant a lot.

The short end of the cigar, its ashes still glowing, bounced along the blacktop, coming to a rest only a few inches from Luthor's front paw. The Doberman began to tremble with excitement, yet still he made no sound.

Crenshaw climbed onto the bike, jumped the engine, and tore off down the block. That used up all the restraint Luthor had. He exploded out of Savannah's embrace and galloped down the sidewalk in pursuit of his beloved Santa, his deafening barks drowned out by the roar of the chopper.

"Luthor—sweetie—come back!" Savannah's cries had no effect on the Doberman, who was at full throttle by now. In desperation, Savannah abandoned her cover and began to sprint down the road after him. But even at top speed, she stood no chance against either a motorcycle or a flying dog. Crenshaw disappeared first. Then Luthor was out of sight, too, popped into nothingness on the horizon.

"Oh, no! Oh, *no!*" Now Luthor was lost, and she had no way to find him. She couldn't even be sure he would catch up to Crenshaw on the motorcycle. What was she going to do?

She pulled out her phone and dialed The Man With The Plan.

13

My butt is frozen to the seat," Ben complained.

"It's not the cold; it's the wind," Pitch insisted. "It cuts right through your coat down to your guts. You really have to bundle up in this kind of weather."

The team, bedecked in coats, hats, and gloves, had taken to their bikes as soon as Savannah had sounded the alarm. Now they were peddling up Ninth Street to rendezvous with their friend and join the search.

"I don't know what you guys are complaining about," Logan said bitterly. "For you it's just miserable. For an actor, getting a scratchy throat could be a career-ender. If I lose my voice, I'll have no chance of impressing Tiffany and her mother and joining the North Shore Players."

"You've got it backward," Pitch informed him. "Losing your voice is only going to help you with Tiffany."

"Tiffany might not be the best judge of character," ventured Melissa. "After all, she has a crush on Darren."

"Quit shivering, Ferret Face," Ben ordered. "You're the one with the fur coat, not me."

"Okay, you guys, I'm cold, too," Griffin admitted. "But if Luthor got lost supporting the plan, then it's part of the plan to help Savannah find him."

"What a surprise," Pitch commented sarcastically. "We're all totally suffering, thanks to a plan. Go figure."

Savannah was waiting for them in front of the Royal Flamingo Suites, her huge eyes still staring down the road where she had last seen Luthor.

At this point, she was nearly frantic and out of breath from running. "My poor sweetie!" she gasped. "I was always afraid that he would follow his big heart into trouble!"

"His big heart isn't the problem," Pitch snapped. "It's his small brain that gave him the idea to fall in love with a Harley-riding Santa."

"Never mind why he did it," Griffin interrupted. "We have to find him. Which way did they go?"

Savannah pointed east along the train line to the industrial area that connected Cedarville with Green Hollow.

The group fanned out, combing the grid of streets, eyes peeled for Dirk Crenshaw's beat-up old motorcycle. Savannah jogged alongside Melissa, stopping every now and then to call, "Luthor!" She was exhausted and winded, but she always found the breath to call for her sweetie.

Ben whizzed up a cross street and came face-to-face with Griffin.

"Is it just me or is this area really scuzzy?" Ben asked in a low voice.

Griffin shivered. "It isn't just you. All the more reason to believe Dirk Crenshaw hangs out here."

At the same instant, both their cell phones pinged. It was a group text from Logan. **Found him. Corner of F Street and Keele Avenue.**

The group converged at that intersection. There was Logan, his bike parked in the shelter of an ancient brick building. It housed the only business on the block that wasn't a pawnshop, a check-cashing place, or an auto body works. A battered sign read:

THE MUG'S MUG
BAR—GRILL—DARTS

Outside, leaning against a NO STANDING sign that had been spray-painted over, were several motorcycles, Crenshaw's among them. All were in various stages of disrepair. Only one had a license plate that hadn't already expired.

"Whoa," said Pitch. "I don't know where the other Santas hang out in their spare time, but this definitely isn't the North Pole."

"Where's Luthor?" Savannah persisted.

Stealthily, Griffin approached the ancient brick building and peered in the flyspecked window. A dense cloud of smoke hung like a fog, obscuring the view of a poorly lit tavern filled with beat-up and mismatched stools, chairs, and tables. About a dozen patrons were spread out between the long bar and a line of dart-boards at the near wall.

Ben sidled up to him. "Which one is Crenshaw?"

Griffin shrugged. "They're all Crenshaw to me." He couldn't quite explain it—the customers at the Mug's Mug didn't look alike exactly. Yet they were all one person: large, tough men with loud voices and bad posture. And they shared the same facial expression—ticked off.

Logan breathed deeply, as if he was standing in a garden of hyacinths. "Wow, look at this place. Talk about gritty reality—sawdust on the floor, human tragedy in the air. These are the life experiences that every actor needs!"

Savannah started for the front door. "If Luthor's in there, I'm going to get him out. It's no place for an innocent animal."

Pitch grabbed her by the arm. "Are you kidding? Luthor's the only one of us with half a chance to survive in that joint!"

"Besides," added Ben urgently, "kids aren't allowed in bars. If my mother caught me in there, I'd be grounded till the next millennium."

"Well, I'm going!" Savannah pulled herself free of Pitch and barreled in through the graffiti-covered door.

The others shared a desperate look, then ran in after her.

Savannah strode purposefully across the tavern, her sneakers kicking up sawdust. "Sweetie! Luthor!"

It caused a stir among the clientele. The Mug's Mug didn't attract many middle schoolers.

At a corner table, a black-jacketed Dirk Crenshaw looked up from a plate of cheese fries. He was surrounded by several companions. The team recognized them from their comings and goings during the former Santa's cigar breaks at the mansion. One of Crenshaw's biker buddies reached down and held out a cheese fry to a familiar expanse of black-and-tan fur.

"Don't eat that!" Savannah called sharply. "It's not good for you!"

She was too late. Luthor wolfed down the offering in a heartbeat.

"Luthor!" As Savannah rushed to admonish her beloved dog, she stepped right in front of a dartboard. One of the players let fly.

Luthor came out from beneath the table like a missile launched from an underground silo. His leap carried him directly into the dart's path, and he snapped it out of the air with bear-trap jaws mere inches before it would have struck Savannah in the side of the head. He hit the sawdust rolling, then got up and trotted to the player, dropping the dart at his feet as if all this had been a game of fetch.

Griffin and the team stood frozen like statues, barely daring to believe what had nearly happened to their friend. The rest of the customers, though, found it the most hilarious thing that had ever happened at the Mug's Mug.

The two dart players were embroiled in a heated argument over whether this counted as a miss or a do-over. Phones came out. Official rulebooks were googled.

"Hey, kid!" Crenshaw called to Savannah. "The mutt is yours, right? He keeps following me!"

"Fried foods and heavy cheeses are not good for a dog's digestion," Savannah lectured Crenshaw and his friends.

"And that's my problem?" Crenshaw demanded. "Keep a leash on him!"

"We'd better grab Savannah," Ben murmured to Griffin, "before we all end up with darts in our skulls!"

"Are you kidding?" crowed Logan. "This place is awesome! I can feel my dramatic range expanding every minute!"

Melissa's curtain of hair stood straight up, her normally beady eyes wide as saucers. She saw something that the others didn't. The darts argument had been growing more and more heated, until the contestants dropped their phones and started throwing punches at each other. A haymaker to the jaw sent one man sprawling into Crenshaw's table, which collapsed. Outraged, Crenshaw and his friends charged into the melee. In seconds, an enormous brawl raged throughout the room.

Griffin and the team dropped to their hands and knees in an attempt to avoid the flying fists. It was no less dangerous down there. Heavy biker boots stomped and broken furniture crashed.

"Luthor!" Savannah admonished. "Get away from those cheese fries!"

"Never mind the cheese fries!" Pitch hollered. "Head for the door! Hurry!"

As the fight raged above and around them, the six middle schoolers crawled through the sawdust and spilled drinks toward the exit. At first, Savannah struggled to keep Luthor with them. The big Doberman seemed concerned about his friend Dirk. Soon, though, it became apparent that Crenshaw's talents included self-defense. Santa Claus could handle himself in a rumble.

They wriggled under a line of mismatched chairs and scrambled to their feet for the run to the exit.

They almost made it.

The door was thrown open, and the Mug's Mug was flooded with police officers.

Griffin looked up and found himself face-to-face with Detective Sergeant Vizzini.

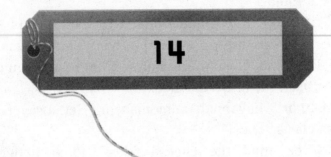

14

So what you're saying," Vizzini leaned over his desk and regarded the six young arrestees seated before him, "is that *you* weren't barhopping. Your dog was."

Savannah spoke up. "He's *my* dog. Well, actually, I don't own him. We're co-equal family members."

"The dog isn't the problem," the policeman informed her. "Dogs can't be underage—like the six of you. Kids aren't allowed in any bar, much less one of the toughest dumps in all of Long Island."

"That's where Luthor comes in," Griffin explained reasonably. "Luthor loves Mr. Crenshaw, so he followed him to the Mug's Mug. Meanwhile, Savannah called us to help her look for her lost dog, and that's where we found him."

Vizzini frowned. "And how does the dog know Crenshaw?"

"That's easy," Logan explained. "Mr. Crenshaw was

Santa Claus in the Colchester Holiday Spectacular. And Luthor was his reindeer."

"They bonded," Savannah added.

"Luthor has a very big heart," Ben supplied, echoing Savannah's words. "You know, along with a very big everything else."

"Are we in a lot of—I mean, how bad is this?" Melissa asked timidly.

Vizzini scribbled in his ring-bound notebook for what seemed like an eternity. "The part that concerns me," he said finally, "is that the Mug's Mug, in addition to being a cesspool, is also a popular meeting spot for people who buy and sell stolen goods. And we happen to have a stolen good—a nearly priceless one—that just went missing in a place where the six of you were all employed. I'd be interested to hear your take on that."

Griffin was horrified. "We didn't steal the Star!"

"That has yet to be determined," the officer informed them. "The first thing you learn at the police academy is that everyone's a suspect until they're not. And so far, nobody's not."

The team exchanged agonized glances. Operation Starchaser was supposed to prove that they were innocent. And all it had done was bring even more suspicion down on them.

They took turns calling home and were picked up by very upset parents. It was one thing to be mixed up in the incident that had brought down the beloved Holiday Spectacular. But getting arrested in the middle of a bar fight at the notorious Mug's Mug was a whole new level of trouble. Blaming it all on the dog would only go so far.

"I'm dead," Ben predicted mournfully. "We're not even allowed to keep Mountain Dew in our house. When my mother finds out I was in a bar, she's going to spray me down with pepperoni juice and feed me to Ferret Face."

At the mention of pepperoni, the little ferret emerged from Ben's collar, looking around hopefully.

"We didn't do anything wrong," Griffin said stoutly. "We searched for a lost dog, that's all. This is no big deal."

But when it was Griffin's turn to call home, there was a lot of yelling on the other end of the line. He held the receiver away from his ear.

Ben was last. As slowly as possible, he dialed his number and prepared for the end of the world.

"Hello, you've reached the Slovaks. No one is available to take your call . . ."

He tried several times, but there was never any answer. So when the Bings arrived to collect their son, Ben was released to them as well.

"I hope you're satisfied, Griffin" was Mr. Bing's harsh greeting as he strapped their bikes onto the station wagon's roof rack. "How many times is this that we've had to pick you up at the police station?"

"Only a few," Griffin replied defensively.

"I'm sorry that our son has gotten you in trouble again," Mrs. Bing added to Ben.

Griffin was insulted. "Hey, we're innocent! All we did was rescue Savannah's dog."

"Don't give me that," Griffin's father snarled. "Savannah's dog doesn't need rescuing. Other people need rescuing from Savannah's dog!"

"Thanks for the ride," Ben told them. "I'm not sure where my parents are, but they'll probably be home soon." He was not looking forward to it.

They turned the corner onto Ben's block. The lights were the first thing they saw. They stretched across the front of the house—big, multicolored, and spinning.

Mrs. Bing stared. "Are those . . . *dreidels?*"

"Oh, boy," Ben breathed. They *were* dreidels. Ben counted fifteen of them dangling from the eaves, rotating slowly. Mr. Slovak perched atop a ladder stringing wires up the wall. He connected the ends of an extension cord and a large menorah lit up, too—with neon candle flames that flashed up and down to create the illusion of motion. The bushes sparkled with six-pointed stars, and a giant latke bearing the message EIGHT NIGHTS OF FUN AND SONG hung dead center on the front door.

Ferret Face poked his head out of Ben's coat to take in the spectacle.

"I guess your dad's really getting into Hanukkah this year," Mr. Bing commented lamely.

"Yeah, Ben, I thought you guys weren't very religious," Griffin put in.

"How religious you are isn't measured by the number of lights you put up," Mrs. Bing reminded her son.

"I just meant that the Slovaks never went all gung ho on Hanukkah before."

Ben was tight-lipped. "I knew what you meant."

The station wagon pulled over to the curb and the passengers stared in amazement. The left side of the house was festooned with the dreidels, the menorah, the latke, and blue and white lights. The right side featured Santa and his reindeer, the snowman, a YULETIDE GREETINGS roof sign, and red and green lights. There was no question about it: Hanukkah on the left and Christmas on the right, with Dad atop the ladder stapling wires on his side and Mom stringing tinsel around the juniper on hers. No wonder no one had answered his phone calls from the police station. They'd been out here the whole time, decorating.

"It looks—nice," Mrs. Bing offered.

Ben could feel his face flushing beet red. It did not look nice. It looked like Christmas and Hanukkah were holding dueling pep rallies across the front of the Slovak home.

Ben and the Bings got out of the car.

"What do you think?" called Mr. Slovak. "Festive, right?"

"It's even more festive on *this* side," his wife countered.

Ben did the only thing he could think of to change the subject.

"Guess what, you guys," he announced. "I got arrested!"

Neither of his parents even heard.

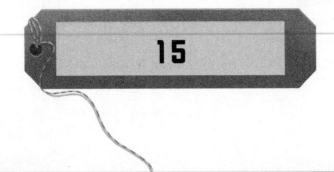

OPERATION STARCHASER-INVESTIGATION NOTES
FIELD AGENT: MELISSA DUKAKIS, CYBER
SURVEILLANCE
SUSPECT: YVETTE BOUCLE

Routine monitoring of suspect's e-mail accounts revealed this message, sent two weeks *before* opening night of the Holiday Spectacular:

"I suppose I pushed Tiffany to join Santa's Workshop so I could be close to the Star. It's the most beautiful thing I've ever seen. If only I could lay my hands on it for even a short time..."

The e-mail was sent to another teacher at the community college. Everyone knows Professor Boucle is working on a book about the Star of Prague. But considering the events of last week, maybe "lay my hands on it" means something a little more sinister....

OPERATION STARCHASER-INVESTIGATION NOTES
FIELD AGENT: GRIFFIN BING, TEAM LEADER
SUSPECT: MR. O'BANNON

Remember that old rust bucket Mr. O'Bannon used to take up to the Colchester mansion when he was working on the Holiday Spectacular? Well, now he's driving a brand-new truck. Business must be good—but how could that be when he just lost Santa's Workshop, his biggest contract?

Maybe it isn't the electrician business that's good. Maybe it's the selling-stolen-art-treasures business.

I'm just thinking—the hose I knelt on in the Colchester toolshed had to have been used recently. Otherwise it wouldn't have still been wet. Who uses an outdoor hose in the middle of winter?

Unless the leaking water that caused the power failure didn't come from melting snow. Maybe it came from that hose.

And who's the one person who would know exactly how to position it so it would drip down to the electrical box? Mr. O'Bannon.

OPERATION STARCHASER-INVESTIGATION NOTES
FIELD AGENT: PITCH BENSON, CLIMBER
SUSPECT: DIRK "FINGERS" CRENSHAW

Melissa gave me a magnetic GPS tracker to stick on Crenshaw's motorcycle. The thing is, Dirk spends a lot of time in the front window, like he's keeping an eye out for somebody. Debt collectors, probably. I don't blame him. Some of those guys look even scarier than he does.

So to keep from getting spotted, I have to free-climb over the apartment building and approach the bike from above. Not a lot of handholds, but luckily the mortar tracks between the bricks are nice and wide. From there, I swing over to a tree, hang by my feet, reach down and snap that sucker on the underside of the fuel tank.

In other words, easy-peasy . . .

OPERATION STARCHASER–INVESTIGATION NOTES
FIELD AGENT: BEN SLOVAK–TIGHT SPACES
SPECIALIST
SUSPECT: DARREN VADER

I was lying in the culvert at the edge of the Vader property, trying to get some pictures inside Darren's room, like you said. But when I looked through the camera viewfinder, I saw this giant orange shape coming at me, growing bigger and bigger until it filled the whole screen. It was that Fruit Armor thingy–your dad's new invention! What kind of patent lawyer lets her rotten kid use an invention to attack people? Seriously, you should rat her out to your dad.

I've got evidence, too–the bump on my head. I'll bet Vader packed the prototype with rocks so it would really hurt. And what about Ferret Face? Ten inches lower and he would have been crushed! Where am I supposed to get another medical service ferret? They don't grow on trees, you know.

I went off on Vader, but all he said was "Way to hang out in the sewer, Slovak." He was laughing too hard for anything more than that. Russell was with him, but at least he kept a straight face. Has that creep ever cracked a smile?

I swear if I have to stay on Vader duty, I'm quitting the team. I don't know if he stole the Star or not, but he's the lowest of the low.

OPERATION STARCHASER-INVESTIGATION NOTES
FIELD AGENT: GRIFFIN BING-TEAM LEADER
SUSPECT: DARREN VADER
Vader's awful, but how can I tell my dad without admitting we've been spying? We'll just have to pray that the prototype doesn't get wrecked until after the patent goes through.

PS: You can't quit, Ben. It's a plan. It's bigger than all of us.

OPERATION STARCHASER-INVESTIGATION NOTES
MELISSA DUKAKIS, CYBER SURVEILLANCE SPECIALIST
SUSPECT: MR. PRIDDLE
I've been monitoring Internet activity on the suspect's personal computer, and I notice he's been spending a lot

of time on the website of Citadel Real Estate in New York City. The thing is, Citadel only sells superexpensive properties—starting at seven or eight million dollars. Where would a personal assistant get that kind of money? Unless he had just gotten hold of something really valuable—something he was about to sell . . .

OPERATION STARCHASER—INVESTIGATION NOTES
FIELD AGENT: LOGAN KELLERMAN, ACTOR
SUSPECT: MISS GRIER

The assignment was to use my acting skills to get a good look inside the Grier house. As usual, I created the perfect character: Ferris Atwater, Junior, a dashing young student selling holiday gift wrap door to door to raise money for his school's drama club.

First things first: My motivation. I had to be so dedicated to selling wrapping paper that I was willing to spend my Christmas break knocking on doors. By the time I got to Miss Grier's, I could feel the role pulsing through my veins. This would be my greatest challenge ever as an actor . . .

OPERATION STARCHASER—INVESTIGATION NOTES
FIELD AGENT: SAVANNAH DRYSDALE, KELLERMAN BACKUP
SUSPECT: MISS GRIER

Don't listen to all that acting mumbo jumbo. While Logan was nice and warm inside with Miss Grier, Luthor and I were freezing our paws off spying on the house from the outside. On a stakeout, you're supposed to be quiet and still, but Dobermans have short coats and need to stay active to keep warm. You'd think someone who calls himself The Man With The Plan would consider something as important as that.

Anyway, Luthor and I were crouched at a window, trying to see inside this wooden chest that might have been the right size to hold the Star, when the door flew open and Miss Grier chased Logan out of the house with a broom.

Honestly, if that was acting, surely a broom upside the head counts as a bad review. Miss Grier missed her calling in life. She's not a Grinch; she's a natural theater critic.

OPERATION STARCHASER-INVESTIGATION NOTES
FIELD AGENT: LOGAN KELLERMAN, ACTOR
SUSPECT: MISS GRIER

What does a dog whisperer know about drama? My acting was fine. The problem was that cheap teapot.

Miss Grier refused to let me in, so I changed the script and said I was authorized to wrap one present for free. I looked around the house as much as I could, but it's not easy to snoop when you're supposed to be wrapping. Trust me—comedy may be hard, but wrapping presents is twenty times harder! The tape gets all messed up, and you drop the scissors, and the paper tears. And when you turn the box over, the top comes off, and this stupid teapot falls on the floor and smashes into a million pieces.

So I said, "I think this one came damaged from the factory." It was a pretty good ad lib, considering I'd been totally caught off guard.

I never found out if Miss Grier stole the Star or not, but she definitely has anger management issues. She picked up the nearest thing at hand—a broom—and started swinging it at me. I responded with another ad lib (running away) which ended this phase of the field assignment.

FINAL NOTE: My shoe came off during my exit, and I couldn't stop and get it. Dramatically, I mean, and also for safety reasons. Savannah went back for it later, but by then, some small animal was living in it, and she wouldn't evict him. So that's on her.

EXPENSE REPORT: 1 Nike sneaker (left), size 8 1/2, slightly used—$40.00.

OPERATION STARCHASER—INVESTIGATION NOTES
FIELD AGENT: GRIFFIN BING, TEAM LEADER
SUSPECT: MISS GRIER
Sorry, Logan. The plan has no budget to pay you back. Besides, how are you going to buy ONE sneaker?

OPERATION STARCHASER—INVESTIGATION NOTES
FIELD AGENT: MELISSA DUKAKIS, CYBER SURVEILLANCE
SUSPECT: DIRK CRENSHAW
I've been monitoring the tracker on the suspect's motorcycle

to see where he goes. He doesn't seem to be employed now that the Holiday Spectacular is shut down. He eats at Szechuan Palace almost every night. He does most of his shopping at 7-Eleven, which is probably where he gets those stinky cigars. He bowls sometimes.

But here's the thing: Every single day, his Harley is parked in front of 14 DeWitt Street for at least a couple of hours. I checked online, and the building is an old tennis racket factory. It can't be his job, though. The place has been closed since the nineties.

Something is going on there, but I can't figure out what.

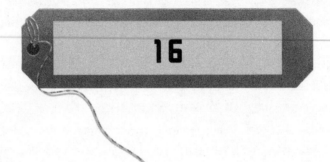

16

Ben gazed up at the fiddler on his roof and wondered how it had come to this.

Ferret Face was looking at the fiddler, too, and cringing from the buzz of the fluorescent lighting. Most of the decorations emitted some sort of power hum, but the fiddler was loudest, rivaling even the inflatable snowman's spotlight, which could sound like a chain saw when the wind blew in the wrong direction.

It had started out innocently enough—an attempt to make up the shortfall in holiday spirit after Santa's Workshop got the ax. Who knew that when Dad saw the Santa, his reindeer, and his sleigh, he'd want equal time for Hanukkah? Or that the sight of all those spinning dreidels and the neon menorah would drive Mom to buy the chorus of angels, the manger, and all those jingle bells?

Now the Slovak house lit up the entire sky over Cedarville. It was beyond embarrassing. It made it practically impossible to get any shut-eye. Even with the blinds drawn, Ben's room was awash with flashing color. It kept Ferret Face up, too—and when Ferret Face didn't sleep, nobody slept. The little creature couldn't comprehend exactly what was wrong, but he knew something was. Alert to a danger that would never come, he twitched all night, gnawing holes in Ben's mattress.

Then there was the music—the bells from the carillon, the carols from the three wise men, and the rousing choruses of "Hava Nagila" and other klezmer favorites coming from the fiddler. Taken individually, there was nothing wrong with any of these. The problem was, they were playing at the same time, warring with one another—the carols coming from the west side of the house, the klezmer from the east, and the bells blasting from behind the chimney.

Ben recognized Griffin's cringe as The Man With The Plan came up the front walk. It was the same neck-into-your-shoulders cringe he'd been seeing on the neighbors these days. Also on the mail carrier and the guy from the power company who came to read the meter and couldn't believe how fast it was spinning. There were zero complaints, though. Nobody wanted to come across as anti-holiday. Which meant that Mom and Dad might never get the message that they were going way off the deep end.

"Is it just me or has it gotten louder?" asked Griffin.

"Dad hooked up a second speaker to the fiddler," Ben confessed miserably. "He was worried the klezmer was getting drowned out by the bells."

"Don't worry. Another week and the holidays will be over."

"I'm pretty sure we're going to have to move after this," Ben predicted. "You know, before we get run out of town."

Griffin laughed appreciatively. "At least you've still got your sense of humor. Now listen. Pitch planted a webcam across from the old tennis racket factory, and Melissa has been monitoring the live feed. Crenshaw and his buddies are in and out of that place every day. We've got to find out what they're doing in there."

"The last time we spied on that guy we wound up arrested in a bar fight," Ben reminded him.

"This is important," Griffin persisted. "It's hard to make progress on Operation Starchaser because we have so many suspects to follow up on. But for all we know, Crenshaw and his biker friends have had the Star of Prague hidden in that factory all along. We've got to get a look around inside there."

"We'd have to break in," Ben reminded him. "I don't think Detective Sergeant Vizzini would like that."

"I wasn't planning to run it by him first," Griffin admitted. "I mean, the company is out of business and the building is abandoned. If Crenshaw and his pals can go in and out of there, why can't we?"

"Because they've got a key?" Ben suggested.

"Okay, so they have a key. But we've got something just as good."

Ben was skeptical. "What's that?"

"A plan."

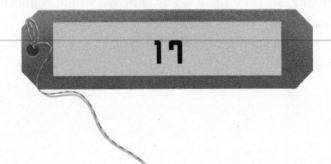

Pitch lay on her bed, her iPad propped against her knees, her mood darkening with every YouTube video. She was watching clips of lucky rock climbers tackling the Red Rocks of Sedona and having a great time doing it. This was *her* trip—the one that the Benson family had planned until everybody had lost their minds and decided she had to be an elf instead. Only now that the elf job had fallen through, it was too late to book Sedona. What a waste! That had to be the worst trade in the world: an amazing climbing trip in exchange for suspicion of Grand Theft Star of Prague.

Seasons greetings.

When the text pinged on her iPad, she was grateful to exit the video. Each beautiful vista, each handhold, foothold, carabiner clip and length of rope, each exhilarated climber added to her despair. This was a winter break she would never get back. Somebody owed her one winter break!

The text was from Melissa, who was monitoring their newest webcam. A one-word message: **NOW**.

Pitch ran downstairs and shrugged into her coat. "I'm going over to Griffin's!" she called, and let herself outside. It was half true. She was headed to the Bing house first, but that was merely the rendezvous point. Their final destination lay on DeWitt Street, number 14—the old tennis racket factory.

It was only 7:15, but this time of year the sky was already full dark. As she passed Ben's block, the glow of the Slovak house caught her eye. It caught everybody's eye these days—everybody within a twenty-mile radius, anyway.

Ben was hurrying down the street, and she paused to let him catch up.

"Your place looks like Las Vegas," she commented.

He nodded in glum agreement and, peering out through the collar of his coat, Ferret Face seemed to nod, too. "And on top of it all, we're in the middle of a plan."

Pitch sighed. "This break is completely trashed. There might as well be a plan to make it interesting. Besides, I'm starting to get kind of curious. Who did steal that dumb Star?"

Griffin was waiting for them at the end of his driveway.

"Where are the others?" Pitch asked.

"It's just us," Griffin told her. "Minimum personnel to reduce the chances of getting caught."

"I hate that word." Ben shivered. *"Caught."*

"Good idea," Pitch agreed, thinking of all six team members under arrest at the Mug's Mug.

Griffin delivered the scouting report. "According to Melissa, the only people who go in and out of that building are Crenshaw and his biker buddies. They left about half an hour ago. This is our chance to see what they're up to. It's definitely some kind of head-quarters. For all we know, the Star is sitting there in plain sight."

Ben looked worried. "What would we do with a ten-million-dollar work of art even if we found it?"

"I don't know what you guys have in mind," Pitch said, "but I vote we march it straight to the police station and shove it up Vizzini's nose. The nerve of that guy, trying to hang this on us. Doesn't he know the first rule of detective work? *The Santa did it.*"

They made their way through neighborhoods, past downtown, to the mostly deserted industrial area near Route 31, then onto DeWitt Street and number 14.

The old building was run-down and seedy, with tall weeds all around it.

Griffin tried the doorknob. Locked.

"I assumed your precious plan was prepared for this situation," Pitch put in.

In answer, Griffin reached into his pocket and produced a hairpin, a nail file, a shrimp fork, a corkscrew, and an expired credit card. He went to work jamming the various implements into the lock while sliding the credit card into the space between the door and the jamb, hoping to flip the bolt. No luck.

Ben was obviously relieved. "Well, we gave it a good try . . ."

"You guys are such dopes." Pitch was already halfway up the building, climbing confidently along an old metal-encased electrical cable. She was moving toward a large high window with several broken panes. When she got there, she reached in, found the latch, and opened it. From there it was a simple matter to swing the window out and insert herself inside. Three minutes later, the factory lights came on. There was the click of a lock and the front door swung wide.

There stood Pitch, inviting them in. "Step into my parlor. Wait till you see what's here."

"Is it the Star?" Griffin asked eagerly. "It's the Star, right?"

"Not exactly."

Pitch led them farther into the factory. Dozens of desks and workbenches had been pushed over to the walls, clearing an area at the center of the large room. Piled there were amplifiers, speakers, a sound mixer, and a variety of musical instruments—three guitars, an electric bass, a keyboard, a tenor saxophone, a trombone, and a large assortment of drums.

Ben looked around. "No Star."

"Maybe not," conceded Griffin. "But this proves that they're a gang of thieves."

"How do you figure that?" asked Pitch.

"Where do you think all this comes from? They must have just hit a music store. Remember what Vizzini said—the Mug's Mug is a hangout for crooks fencing stolen goods. They must warehouse the swag here until they find a buyer."

Ben was skeptical. "I don't know, Griffin. This stuff looks pretty expensive, but the Star of Prague is supposed to be worth ten million dollars. If you have something that valuable, why would you bother with this junk?"

Pitch had a theory. "It's only worth ten million if you can find someone who wants to pay it. Not a lot of people have that kind of money. You saw the Mug's Mug. You think anybody in that dump has ten million bucks? So while they're waiting for some super-rich zillionaire to come and buy the Star, they still have to pay the bills. And they keep on stealing."

"Do you think the Star could be sold already?" mused Ben.

"I doubt it," Griffin replied. "Crenshaw and his gang were here as recently as half an hour ago. If you had ten million bucks, would you be wasting your time in a place like this?"

Pitch wrinkled her nose. "If I had that kind of money, I'd hire a cleaning lady." She indicated the floor around the instruments, which was littered with fast-food containers, snack wrappers, and cigar butts. "Santa Slob is going to end up on his own naughty list."

The three invested a few minutes searching the

factory space for anything that might have been hiding the Star. It would have been a tragedy to overlook the priceless artwork just because it was inside a burlap sack or behind a stack of boxes. But there was no sign of it. Except for the instruments and related gear, the building contained nothing but old office furniture and equipment, a few startled mice, and dust, dust, dust.

The three friends were heading for the exit when the door flew open and in stalked a young bodybuilder type, with a shaved head and muscles that showed through his heavy leather jacket. Spying the middle schoolers, he frowned, bringing half his bald head down to his brow.

"Where's Fingers?" he asked.

Griffin was the only one who still had a voice. "He's—uh—not in right now. Can I take a message?"

"Who are you three, and what are doing here?" The newcomer's eyes narrowed as they focused on Griffin. "Are you Fingers's kid?"

Please tell me I don't look like him! Griffin's mind was racing. His first thought had been that one of Crenshaw's pals had walked in on them. But none of that gang was this young, this bald, or this muscular. And yet, the intruder was definitely familiar. Griffin had seen him somewhere before. But where?

The newcomer interpreted Griffin's terrified silence as a yes. "Don't worry—I'm not going to hurt you. You shouldn't have to suffer just because your old man's a deadbeat. But you tell him this: Gustave says what he owes is getting out of hand and taking too long. There are going to be consequences."

All at once, Griffin realized where he'd seen the bald muscleman before. Outside the Colchester mansion, during one of Crenshaw's many cigar breaks, this threatening visitor had appeared several times—always demanding payment to settle gambling debts.

"Your old man told me he was coming into mad cheddar around Christmas," the enforcer went on. "That's now. Where's the cash?"

"I—I—I'll tell him," Griffin stammered.

"Either I get paid, or it's an unhappy ending all around. Make sure he knows that." He glanced out the window at the litter-strewn street and added, "You kids should go home. You run into a lot of creeps in this neighborhood." He stormed out, slamming the door behind him. Seconds later, they heard a high-powered engine and the squeal of tires pulling away.

"Man," reflected Pitch, "Dirk Crenshaw may be a big jerk, but I feel sorry for him. How'd you like to have Gustave mad at you?"

"Save your sympathy," Griffin advised. "You heard what he said—Crenshaw told him he'd be coming into 'mad cheddar.' That means money. He's got the Star."

"Shouldn't we warn him?" asked Ben. "Star or not, I'd want to know if some big scary cue ball was coming to give me an unhappy ending."

"We can't," Pitch insisted. "Not without admitting we've been snooping around his hideout."

"I agree," said Griffin. "It's not our problem that Crenshaw's got himself in trouble with dangerous people."

"It is if he tells Gustave that he doesn't have a son, and Gustave comes looking for us," Ben quavered.

Griffin stared at him. "You think too much. Let's get out of here. We need to adjust the plan. The other suspects are on the back burner. From now on, we focus on Fingers."

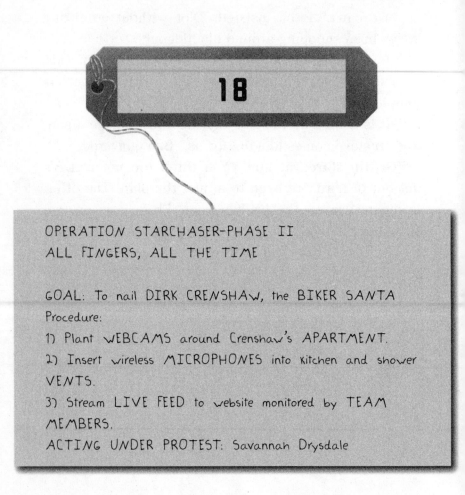

OPERATION STARCHASER-PHASE II
ALL FINGERS, ALL THE TIME

GOAL: To nail DIRK CRENSHAW, the BIKER SANTA
Procedure:
1) Plant WEBCAMS around Crenshaw's APARTMENT.
2) Insert wireless MICROPHONES into kitchen and shower
VENTS.
3) Stream LIVE FEED to website monitored by TEAM
MEMBERS.
ACTING UNDER PROTEST: Savannah Drysdale

Griffin sighed. Savannah was hanging on to her theory of Crenshaw's innocence. In her opinion, Luthor's devotion was better than any lie-detector test. Fingers couldn't be guilty, because Luthor could never love a crook.

Griffin hoped she'd give her all to the next phase of the plan. The team could not sacrifice even one pair of eyes and ears for this kind of surveillance blitz.

He checked his phone, which showed a split-screen display of the various camera feeds and played audio from the two microphones. What if nobody was watching or listening when Crenshaw revealed where he'd stashed the Star? Of course, Melissa was also recording everything. But with a career criminal like Crenshaw, they'd have to act fast. He'd never leave such a hot item exposed for very long.

The sound of running water came from the phone's small speaker. And was that *singing*?

Singing in the shower definitely didn't fit Crenshaw's profile as a master thief. Come to think of it, showering at all was kind of surprising for such a slob. No more surprising than a part-time job as a Santa Claus. But he'd only taken *that* to get close to the Star of Prague.

Griffin silenced his phone and headed downstairs. He found his father pacing the kitchen, his face careworn.

"Everything okay, Dad?"

Mr. Bing slumped in a chair. "Daria Vader isn't taking my calls."

Griffin took a seat across from him. "Maybe she lost her phone."

"It's the landline she uses for her law practice," Mr. Bing replied sadly. "She's not answering my e-mails, either."

"Take a drive over there," Griffin suggested.

His father shook his head. "It won't do any good. There's a problem with the new patent application. I can feel it."

"But you tested Fruit Armor," Griffin reminded him. "It worked perfectly. The golf club, remember?"

"In order to be awarded a patent, an invention has to do more than just work," Mr. Bing explained. "It has to be unique, and it has to perform a worthwhile function. Mrs. Vader's a good lawyer, but she's a stickler. She's not always the easiest person to deal with."

"That runs in some families," Griffin commented, thinking of Darren.

He eased his phone out of his pocket and snuck a look at it under the table. Crenshaw, now wrapped in an old bathrobe and puffing on a cigar, came padding outside, carrying an overstuffed garbage bag. He tossed it at the trash bin and missed. The thin plastic broke apart, spewing chicken bones, candy wrappers, and banana peels all over the ground. He stared at the mess for a moment, shrugged, turned around, and padded back into the building.

It was hard evidence that the former Santa was a pig. What they needed was evidence he was a criminal.

Come on, Fingers. Where did you hide the Star?

They were on the right track—Griffin was sure of it. They just had to wait for the thief to make a mistake.

* * *

The faded black-and-white photograph showed a boy of about twelve, blond and beaming, in the Great Hall of the Colchester mansion.

A boy of *exactly* twelve, Charles Colchester corrected himself. He knew this, because the child was himself in 1947, the first year he'd been an elf in his grandfather's Holiday Spectacular.

Mr. Colchester remembered the exhilarating details of that old pageant as if it had happened only yesterday. The world had just come through a terrible depression, followed by a terrible war, but all that disappeared the instant you stepped into the Great Hall. As you stood beneath the towering tree with the Star of Prague at its peak, all your cares were carried away, replaced by music and celebration, food, drink, and fun.

A wave of melancholy swept over the patriarch of the Colchester family. The long-standing tradition of Santa's Workshop had survived wars, depressions, storms, labor disputes, flu epidemics, and even the year the tree had been struck by freak lightning aboard the flatbed truck that was bringing it down from Maine. Was the loss of the Star of Prague—devastating as it was—worse than World War II? Did it warrant selling this wonderful old mansion on Long Island Sound and leaving Cedarville, which had been home to Colchesters for more than a century and a half?

It wasn't even the financial loss. The Star had been insured with Lloyd's of London. It was the betrayal—

the fact that one of his *neighbors* had taken what was so much a symbol of the Colchesters. The family had given so much to the community, and *this* was their reward. For Charles Colchester, there was no getting past it.

The police were doing everything possible, but still could not reassure him that the Star would ever be recovered. It was as if the Star had disappeared into thin air.

There was a knock at the door of the study, and Priddle entered. Ah, loyal Priddle—what would Mr. Colchester have done without his trusted assistant throughout these dark days?

"Sir, I have a message from your son and daughter-in-law in the Galápagos. They'll be returning home soon, and have arranged for young Russell to fly back to California on the night of the twenty-fourth."

"Christmas Eve," Mr. Colchester mused glumly. "So not even Russell will be here for Christmas."

"That must be very disappointing, sir," Priddle offered.

"Just one of many disappointments this year. But facts must be faced. I wanted to share the Holiday Spectacular with my grandson. Now that's off, so there's nothing to share."

A volley of running footsteps sounded from downstairs.

"*Walk*, boys!" Priddle called over his shoulder. To his employer, he explained, "That would be Russell and his friend Darren looking for snacks in the kitchen. Boys that age are bottomless pits."

Mr. Colchester nodded. Darren, who was ample, to say the least, was the bottomless pit. He was not the sort of company Mr. Colchester would have chosen for Russell. But he had to admit he was glad that his grandson had someone to "hang out" with, as the young people put it. It was pretty plain that Russell wasn't too fond of Cedarville. So much for the hope that a role in Santa's Workshop would change his mind on that.

Perhaps it was just as well that the boy was going home.

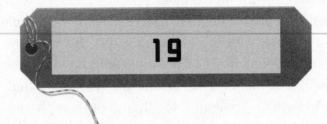

19

"Would you mind hurrying it up, Logan?" Mr. Kellerman demanded impatiently. "You've been sitting there for ten minutes. Pick a color and let's go."

Logan sat in front of the lighted mirror at Theatricality, his favorite performers' supply store. With a cosmetic sponge, he applied a dab of makeup to his left cheek and compared it to the dab on his right. "Still not perfect." He rubbed it all off, rinsed the sponges, and started again.

"Logan . . ." his father warned.

"You know, the least you could do is be patient, Dad," Logan said irritably. "I inherited my weak chin from you. If I can't find the right shade to build it up, I'll never ace my audition with the North Shore Players when I get it."

Mr. Kellerman exhaled in exasperation. "Five minutes, and not a second longer. My weak chin and I will be waiting for you at the cash register." He started away.

"Pick up a copy of *Backstage* magazine while you're over there," Logan called after him. He tried another makeup color. Better, but not quite there.

A sound reached him then—a young girl's voice singing "O Holy Night." She was good. No, better than good—fantastic. And strangely familiar . . .

He spotted Tiffany Boucle standing by a rack of sheet music. She wasn't singing, though. It was her voice, but the music was coming from the phone in her hand.

He rushed over to join her. "Wow, Tiffany. That's awesome!" He meant it, too, and not just because her mother could get him into the North Shore Players.

Well, maybe a little bit because of that. But she really *was* awesome.

"Oh, hi, Logan. Thanks. My mom recorded it and posted it to YouTube." She held out the screen, which showed her in a red party dress, singing in front of a roaring fire.

"This is my favorite store," Logan enthused. "I get all my stage makeup here. And their costumes are good, too."

"I'm looking for a new song to perform at the North Shore Players' holiday party. Mom's going to let me do a couple of numbers."

Logan bit his tongue. He'd have given anything to be at that party, but these days he was on Yvette Boucle's Least Wanted list. "Well, if the video is any indication, you're going to blow everybody away."

She looked grateful for a moment. Then two small tears began to roll down her pale cheeks.

Logan was horrified. "Why are you crying? I said you were great!"

"Not *you*!" she blubbered. "When I showed the clip to Darren, he told me I sounded like—like—like some poor dinosaur caught in the tar pits!"

"I don't think they had tar pits in the time of the dinosaurs," Logan pointed out.

"He didn't mean it literally!" she exploded. "He thinks I stink. I've done everything I could think of to catch Darren's attention, and he treats me like I'm—like I'm—"

"Pond scum?" Logan suggested helpfully.

Tiffany only cried harder.

"Well," Logan explained reasonably, "that's because Darren Vader is a terrible person. If you'd grown up in Cedarville instead of Green Hollow, you'd already know that."

He thought it would make her feel better. Instead, she became even more distressed. "How dare you say that about Darren! He may be a little rough on the outside, but deep down I know he's sweet and funny and caring and wonderful! I like him *so* much . . ." She fell silent, overcome with emotion.

Logan stared at her perfect heart-shaped face. She wasn't kidding. Her moist, puffy eyes were wide with sincerity. She honestly felt this strongly about *Vader*!

Unbelievable! How unfair was that?

Logan remembered an acting workshop he'd once taken in New York City. "You must explain your character's motivation for all things except one," the teacher had lectured. "Love. There is no rational reason why one person falls for another. It simply happens."

It was not logical, the man had concluded. But it was absolutely human.

In other words, I shouldn't be offended at all that Tiffany prefers an obnoxious lunkheaded oaf who treats her like garbage over me. She's just being human.

That gave Logan an idea.

"You're right," he soothed. "That's just Darren's tough exterior. Inside he's really"—Logan nearly gagged over the word—"nice."

"Do you honestly think so?" Tiffany asked earnestly.

"I don't just think it—I'm positive," Logan assured her. "And as your friend, I promise to do my best to make sure that great guy comes to see what a great girl he's got in you."

She brightened, and Logan understood that he had said exactly the right thing. If he kept this up, he'd be in the North Shore Players before he knew it.

The young actor realized he was now facing the most difficult and challenging role of his career: somebody who *didn't* believe Darren Vader was evil.

Ben was outraged.

The e-veterinarian website had an awful lot to say about dogs, cats, hamsters, and parakeets. So how come Ben's search for "ferret stress disorder" had turned up zero matches? They had articles about ESP in rabbits and alpacas with learning disabilities, but nothing to explain why a perfectly healthy ferret in the prime of life was nervous and jumpy and couldn't relax.

Ben sat back from the desk and sighed. He didn't need the Internet to tell him why Ferret Face was a wreck—it was the same reason Ben himself was so anxious. The hum and buzz of a bazillion lights got into your whole body and settled in your spleen, wherever that was. Even in the middle of the night, when everything was shut off, the memory of it was still with you.

The vibration of the lights outside the Slovak home was still easier to handle than the vibration of the tension inside it. What had begun with Dad's concern that his family's Hanukkah traditions might be lost in the glitz of a big Christmas display had turned into a full-on decoration war. And Ben was caught in the middle.

First it had been the sniping back and forth over whose strings of lights were sagging off the eaves, or whether the glowing reindeer or the dancing fiddler was most responsible for the Slovaks' ballooning electric bill. Soon, though, Mom and Dad had stopped talking to each other altogether. Now all communication between them flowed through Ben:

"Benjamin, tell your father that the blown capacitor for *his* menorah is sapping power from the air compressor for *my* snowman."

"I'm sure your mother already knows that the only reason my capacitor blew was because of the faulty wiring between Comet and Cupid."

No wonder poor Ferret Face was frazzled.

The grinding of a large motor drew his attention out the window. A large semitrailer was backing up to the house. His father was there, too, supervising the unloading of a huge crate that might easily have contained a refrigerator or a small tractor. It took two men and Dad to get it off the truck and onto the Slovaks' front lawn.

Ben ran downstairs and burst out the front door, the discordant mix of bells and carols from one end of the property and klezmer music from the other clashing painfully inside his head. "What's that, Dad? What's a"—he squinted at the markings on the box—"drei-dirigible?"

"Your mother thinks she has me outgunned," Mr. Slovak chortled triumphantly. "Every time I put up a few blue lights or an extra latke, she can just hop online and bury me under a mountain of candy canes and holly. Well, let's see her try to bury *this*."

With a sinking heart, Ben examined the illustration

on the packaging. The drei-dirigible was a dreidel-shaped hot-air balloon that hovered over the house, blinking HAPPY HANUKKAH in LED letters. When Mom saw this . . .

The expression that jumped to mind came from Dad's side of the family: *Oy vey.*

"Make sure you secure it to the roof nice and tight," the driver of the semi was telling Mr. Slovak. "I've seen these suckers fly away on people. They just keep going until the propane burns out, forty, fifty miles away. Can you tie a barrel hitch?"

"I almost made it to Eagle Scout," Ben's father replied confidently.

Ben and Ferret Face watched dubiously as Mr. Slovak signed the delivery bill and the truck roared away.

"Dad—this is crazy," Ben pleaded. "We always celebrated both holidays just fine. We never needed reindeer and fiddlers and snowmen and drei-dirigibles."

"I didn't start this," Mr. Slovak said righteously.

Ben watched his father walk off in search of a toolbox. Dad was right. He hadn't started it. Neither had Mom. This whole Christmas-versus-Hanukkah arms race had begun the night Dirk Crenshaw stole the Star of Prague. That was what made Charles Colchester cancel the Holiday Spectacular, which inspired Estelle Slovak and a handful of local moms to step up their own home displays.

This was Crenshaw's fault!

Griffin's plans always seemed crazy at first, but now Ben was behind Operation Starchaser 100 percent. If they caught the thief and recovered the Star, maybe—just maybe—Mr. Colchester could be persuaded to reopen Santa's Workshop, which would take the holiday heat off of everybody.

It might be the only way to save the Slovak family.

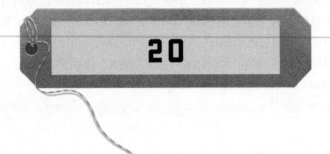

20

The Drysdale home contained the largest number of animals of any place on Long Island not officially designated an animal shelter, wildlife preserve, or zoo.

Savannah's housemates—never say pets—included cats, rabbits, hamsters, guinea pigs, a pack rat, a capuchin monkey, and an albino chameleon. They shared equal status with the human Drysdales and one another.

Unofficially, though, Luthor was always a little more equal than everybody else.

The big Doberman had the run of the house. He was first in the kitchen, got the choicest table scraps, and enjoyed top priority when it came to drinking out of the toilet. No one would dream of changing the channel when he was watching Animal Planet, and he was adept at using his large black snout to jiggle Savannah's computer out of screen saver mode, even though the mouse usually wound up on the floor and the mouse pad would be covered in drool.

Savannah and her parents were just finishing dinner when the familiar clunk of the mouse was followed by an eruption of deep-throated barking that could only come from one source.

"God bless America!" moaned Mr. Drysdale. "Savannah, go quiet your dog."

"He's not *my* dog any more than I'm *his* person," Savannah reminded her father as she left the table and started up the stairs.

Savannah's room was bedlam. Luthor was leaping like a puppy, his head coming dangerously close to smacking into the ceiling. Cleopatra, the monkey, cowered atop a bookcase, trying to stay out of the line of fire. Lorenzo, the chameleon, would have been turning all sorts of colors, except that he was albino and had to stay white. Rosencrantz and Guildenstern, the cats, peered out from under the bed, waiting for Luthor to calm down.

Luthor was anything but calm, and Savannah soon saw the reason. The computer broadcast a split-screen view from all of Melissa's webcams. One of them showed Dirk Crenshaw in front of his apartment.

"Oh, sweetie, I know what's got you so excited. It's your friend Santa!"

She manipulated the mouse and clicked to bring the image of Crenshaw to full screen. This sent Luthor into waves of joy, rolling on the floor, rubbing his belly against the rug.

Savannah looked a little closer at the image on the

monitor. Crenshaw was struggling to strap an awkward case onto the back of his motorcycle. It was round, battered black leather, and it didn't quite close properly because the clips were broken. A gap opened up as he tried to secure it shut with bungee cords. Whatever was inside caught the beam of a streetlight and sparkled.

"The Star of Prague!" Savannah breathed, her exhilaration tempered by a pang of regret. Poor, sweet, trusting Luthor was going to be devastated when he found out that Crenshaw was nothing but a common crook. Of course, a canine brain could never wrap itself around the *legal* idea of guilt and innocence. But a sensitive creature like Luthor would understand that the Santa he loved was a fallen man in deep disgrace. And the Doberman would certainly notice his friend's absence if the thief had to do prison time.

Heart pounding, she Skyped Melissa. The shy girl came on immediately, her curtain of hair parted, her beady eyes alight with discovery. "I saw it, too!"

"It's the Star, isn't it?" Savannah rasped.

"What else could it be?" Melissa reasoned. "I've been trying to reach Griffin, but he isn't online."

"Call the others," Savannah urged.

A moment later, Logan's face intruded on their conversation. "I'm busy, you guys," he said in annoyance. "I'm editing a music video for Tiffany Boucle."

"Don't lie, Logan," Savannah snapped. "Tiffany hates you."

"Not anymore," Logan reported smugly. "I've figured out the key to her heart. All I have to do is say good things about Vader."

"There are no good things about Vader," Savannah insisted.

"Never mind that," Melissa interrupted. "Check out the live feed from Crenshaw's webcam. What do you think of that?"

"It's suspicious, all right," Logan agreed. "He shaved. He never shaves!"

"Not his face!" Savannah exploded. "Look at the case on the back of his motorcycle. Something shiny is inside—something just about the size of the Star of Prague."

At that moment, Pitch joined the Skype call, her image unsteady. "What's going on?"

"Where are you?" Melissa asked.

Pitch's expression turned sheepish. "On the roof of my house. I had to climb something. I'm *entitled* to climb something. I'm supposed to be at Red Rocks, climbing something! Hey, did you guys know there's some kind of hot-air balloon flying right over Cedarville? It says something on the side, but I can't read it."

Ben's fuzzy image appeared beside the others. "It's the drei-dirigible. Don't ask. It says 'Happy Hanukkah,' but you might be facing the side where it's written in Hebrew."

"Ben, I can hardly see you," Savannah told him. "What's wrong with your computer?"

"It could be the magnetic field created by all the lights around Ben's house," Melissa suggested. "Everybody check the webcam on Crenshaw's apartment. We think he's making a move with the Star of Prague."

"What?" It was Griffin, online at last. And when he examined the webcam feed, his features tightened into a mixture of satisfaction and determination. Operation Starchaser was entering its final phase.

"All right, you guys," said The Man With The Plan. "This is it. Tonight we nab the Bad Santa and bring home the Star of Prague."

"How do we do that?" asked Ben. "We call the police, right?"

"Not yet," Griffin replied. "Not till we know exactly where he's taking it."

"We've got that GPS on his Harley," put in Melissa.

In the live feed, Crenshaw climbed onto the motorcycle, jumped it to life, and roared off. The six team members caught one final gleam from the contents of the round case before the former Santa disappeared offscreen.

"To your bikes, everybody!" Griffin ordered. "We'll track the GPS on our phones."

Every one of Griffin's plans had a moment like this one. He spoke the words he had said to them many times before.

"It's zero hour."

21

Zero felt more like the temperature than the hour as the team pedaled out into the winter night, shivering under coats, hats, and gloves. The actual number was in the mid-thirties, but with the sun down, it seemed even colder than the day they had tailed Crenshaw to the Mug's Mug.

They came from different directions, converging on Ninth Street, Cedarville's main drag. Griffin sped up to pull even with Pitch, in the lead.

The young climber was an elite athlete, but even she was struggling to keep her breathing steady as the frigid air burned her lungs. "I hope somebody knows where we're going."

"I do," Melissa panted, indicating her smartphone, which glowed in the basket of her old-fashioned Schwinn. The small screen showed a red pulsing dot moving through the street grid. "That's the tracker on Crenshaw's motorcycle."

"Don't lose it," Griffin said grimly.

"He's on a *Harley*," Ben reminded them. "We're on *bikes*. What if he's going to New Jersey? Or California?"

"This better not be a false alarm," complained Logan, teeth chattering. "A sniffle can be death to an actor at an audition."

"Good thing nobody's crazy enough to give you an audition," Pitch tossed over her shoulder at him.

"Are you kidding? My Vader strategy is totally working! Tiffany will be talking me up to her mom before you can say 'Stanislavski.'"

Griffin bumped over a pothole. "It can't be a false alarm. We all saw Crenshaw strap the Star onto his motorcycle."

"There's more," Melissa added. "I checked the other webcams before leaving the house. Guess what was on the one across from the old tennis racket factory? His buddies are carrying out all those instruments and loading them into a van."

Ben frowned. "Doesn't it seem kind of weird that you'd sell a bunch of used musical instruments to the same buyer who can afford a ten-million-dollar work of art?"

Griffin was annoyed. "That's so typical of you, Ben. Why are you looking for problems that don't exist? The plan is coming together. This is the real thing!"

Savannah was the last to join the procession, Luthor loping at her side.

"Why'd you bring the dog?" Griffin demanded. "If he gets too loud, Crenshaw will figure out we're onto him."

"Luthor has as big a stake in this as any of us," Savannah reasoned.

"Luthor *eats* as big a steak as any of us," Pitch amended. "As for the other kind of stake, he doesn't have one. He's a dog."

"He gave his heart to Dirk Crenshaw," Savannah explained. "He needs to see the man he admired arrested and hauled off to jail. It'll be a tough lesson for him, but it'll teach him to be more careful about where he places his trust. How else will he grow?"

"I hope he doesn't grow," Ben said fervently. "He's already the biggest Doberman in history. If he gets any bigger, he's a *T. Rex.*"

Melissa's quiet voice interrupted the conversation. "He stopped."

It took a moment for everyone to realize what she meant: The tracker on Crenshaw's motorcycle had come to a halt.

Griffin peered at the phone in Melissa's basket. "He's at the corner of Washington and Route Thirty-One. What's there?"

"There's Armando's Deli," Ben supplied. "That's where they make Ferret Face's favorite pepperoni. But there's no place to pull off a ten-million-dollar deal."

"Wait—false alarm," Melissa reported. "He's moving again. He must have just been held up at a light."

"I knew it," Ben mourned. "He's on his way to Jersey."

"All his contacts have been local," Griffin argued. "We can't give up now. Not when we're so close."

They continued their ride in silence, all eyes on the pulsing dot on Melissa's phone. They pedaled hard, partly to keep from falling too far behind, but mostly because the physical effort helped them keep warm. The blustery wind found every opening in their coats. Their feet felt like blocks of ice. As they were passing Armando's, Ferret Face wiggled his way up through Ben's scarf, but quickly ducked back down again. Not even the delectable smell of pepperoni was worth braving the cold.

They crossed Route 31 and had not gone very far when Melissa announced, "He's stopped again. And this time he's pulled off the road a little. I think he's there."

"Where?" Griffin asked anxiously.

"About two miles ahead of us. The GPS says it's Seventeen Five-Fifty South Washington."

Griffin pulled over to the side of the road, and the others joined him on the shoulder. He took out his own phone and dialed the Cedarville Police Department. "This is an urgent message for Detective Sergeant Vizzini . . . Never mind my name . . . Tell the detective that if he wants to find the Star of Prague, he has to come right now to Seventeen Five-Fifty South Washington Avenue. The deal could be going down any minute." He broke the connection.

Pitch regarded him with respect. "I know I get on your case sometimes, Griffin, but you really are The Man With The Plan."

The others nodded their agreement.

"Thanks, you guys," Griffin said in a husky voice. "Now let's go. We want to get there just ahead of the cops."

They rode south past several strip malls, keeping track as the address numbers counted down from eighteen thousand. At first Griffin thought that Crenshaw's destination was one of these plazas, and that the exchange would take place in the parking lot, or perhaps out back. But they crested a rise, and there it was—a low building behind a fluorescent sign.

AMERICAN LEGION HALL
NORTH SHORE POST #466

"American Legion?" Melissa's curtain of hair stood straight out, buffeted by wind and bewilderment. "Like—veterans? What would *they* want with the Star of Prague?"

"It's not the legionnaires themselves," Griffin concluded. "Crenshaw and his gang are just using their place to make the exchange."

The six abandoned their bikes at the end of the driveway and stole toward the parking lot, which was full of cars.

"Look—" hissed Logan. "Crenshaw's Harley."

"And that's the van I saw," added Melissa, pointing.

They searched the lot. No one was in any of the vehicles making a ten-million-dollar deal.

"They must be inside the Legion Hall," Pitch decided.

"I think there's a party going on in there," mused Savannah. "Does anybody else hear music?"

Griffin set his jaw. "It's the perfect setup. People are eating, drinking, and dancing; the music covers all sound; and the bad guys are in the back room, selling a priceless art treasure."

Logan was inspired. "We might get a medal for this."

"I'd settle for not being blamed anymore for stealing the Star," Ben put in sourly. "And it would be nice to get home alive tonight, too."

Over the music, the wail of police sirens reached them—distant, but growing louder.

Griffin nodded with satisfaction. "Perfect timing. Let's get in there. I can't wait to see the look on Vizzini's face when he has to admit we were right and he was wrong."

Savannah tied Luthor's leash around a light stand, and the group hurried toward the front door of the Legion Hall.

The knob felt cold in Griffin's hand, even through his glove—or maybe it was the nervous exhilaration of a plan coming to its triumphant payoff.

He opened the door and the group trooped inside. Savannah was right. There *was* a party going on, some sort of holiday celebration. Shiny decorations adorned the walls, and delectable aromas came from a line of buffet tables. Everywhere, people were dancing, chatting in groups, and helping themselves to dinner.

Ferret Face hoisted himself up onto Ben's shoulder, his needle nose twitching. With a joyous leap, he abandoned his post and dashed to the food line, snapping up fallen scraps from the diners.

"Get back here, Ferret Face—" Ben made a move to follow, but froze when his eyes fell on the low platform stage.

They all did. One by one, the jaws dropped.

The song was "Rock Around the Clock," an old classic rock-and-roll song from the fifties. But it was not the rockabilly tune that caught their attention; it was the band members themselves.

Griffin and his friends had seen them all before— riding their motorcycles, having lunch at the Mug's Mug, visiting their buddy for long cigar breaks outside the Colchester mansion.

That buddy was in the band, too—in fact, he was the lead singer.

Dirk Crenshaw.

22

The former Santa Claus stood center stage, the pick in his hand just a blur on the strings of his electric guitar. His massive form was graceful, almost catlike, as he crooned into the microphone.

His biker bandmates jammed energetically along, banging out the lively rock-and-roll song. And their instruments were the "stolen" instruments from the tennis racket factory.

A banner behind them blazoned the name of the group:

FINGERS AND THE FLYTRAPS

Fingers, Griffin thought in agony. A nickname for a thief—or a guitarist. And the singing in the shower—practice!

"I can't believe it!"

"I know," put in Logan. "Who would have guessed

that Dirk Crenshaw was such a talented performer? But where does the Star of Prague come in?"

"It doesn't, Einstein!" Pitch exploded. "Crenshaw and his buddies didn't steal those instruments, either. They're a band! The tennis racket factory must be where they rehearse!"

"No way!" Ben rasped in astonishment. "We saw him pack the Star inside that case!"

"We didn't, you know," Melissa mused thoughtfully. "We saw something shiny that was the right size and shape, so we assumed it was the Star. But—"

They scoured the hall until, at last, the six of them were staring straight up. They gawked. They goggled.

A gleaming disco ball hung from the ceiling, sparkling in the spotlights as it turned slowly.

"No," moaned Savannah. "No, no, no."

"Okay, nobody panic," Griffin said, struggling to keep his own panic under control. "We've hit Code Z, that's all."

Every plan had a Code Z built into it—the moment when an operation was damaged beyond saving and all that remained was to get out of there.

They wheeled and headed for the exit, only to come face-to-face with a police officer.

"Nobody goes in or out!" the man bellowed. "This building is under lockdown!"

The music came to a crashing halt. Fingers and the Flytraps stood stock-still, openmouthed, as more uniforms appeared. Dozens of startled party guests turned toward the doorway, wondering what had put an end to their festivities.

"Why has the music stopped?" The event's hostess stepped forward to investigate the interruption. It was Yvette Boucle.

Logan frowned. "What's *she* doing here?"

"Uh-oh." Savannah directed her friend's attention to a sign prominently displayed on a tripod.

WELCOME TO THE NORTH SHORE PLAYERS' YULETIDE AND HOLIDAY SOCK HOP

"Wow." Logan was pleased. "I was dying to come to this."

"As a *guest*," Pitch amended. "Not the guy who brought the cops in to raid the place."

Logan went white and tried to duck behind the much shorter Ben.

Too late. "Logan?" This came from Tiffany.

"Logan?" Mrs. Boucle's eyes narrowed. "Officers, exactly what is going on here? Who's responsible for this intrusion?"

"That would be me," came a deep, commanding voice from the doorway. In strode Detective Sergeant Vizzini. "These premises are subject to search. We have reason to believe the Star of Prague might be—" His eyes fell on Griffin and the team and the words died on his lips.

"Uh—about that," Griffin stammered. "The information, I mean. We thought—I mean, *I* thought—"

Vizzini's mouth hardened into a thin line. "That tip was from you, wasn't it?"

"There was a little misunderstanding." Griffin pointed up at the disco ball. "We thought *that*—well, you know how it's the right size, and the right shape, and kind of sparkly—"

The tall detective was under tight control. "The Star of Prague is worth ten million dollars. That thing goes for nineteen ninety-five at Walmart."

"We were only trying to help," Logan offered meekly.

"I know exactly what you were trying to do!" Mrs. Boucle raged. "You've been trying to wrangle an invitation to this party from day one. Well, I've got news for you, Logan Kellerman. You will *never* see that invitation, because you will *never* be a part of the North Shore Players!"

"Does that include summer stock?" Logan asked earnestly.

"It includes *everything*!" she bawled. "I wouldn't hire you to sweep mothballs out of the costume room! If an asteroid hit the earth and you were the last actor left alive, I'd cast a baboon rather than give the job to you!"

Vizzini stepped in. "Obviously, you two have your own issues, which are not police business. But as for this so-called tip, do you kids realize that feeding false information to the police is a crime?"

"We only found out it was false a minute ago," offered Savannah.

Griffin stepped forward. "Everybody in town suspects we've got something to do with stealing the Star. We thought this was a chance to prove we were innocent and get the Star back at the same time. Okay, it didn't work out that way, but that would have been a good thing, right?"

"Don't you see that when I make my report on this, it'll look like you deliberately led us on a wild-goose chase? You're digging yourselves a very deep hole."

Griffin opened his mouth to protest and shut it again at a warning look from Pitch. Vizzini was right: Everything they said, everything they did to prove themselves innocent, only made them look guiltier.

The silence that followed was punctuated by a gurgling snore from below. Without Ferret Face keeping his narcolepsy at bay, Ben had collapsed into a cross-legged sleep on the floor. Griffin gave him a gentle nudge with his toe.

Ben opened one eye. "What?" He took stock of his surroundings and scrambled to his feet. A guilty-looking Ferret Face, still munching on a piece of salami, ran up his leg and disappeared under his coat.

"Can we go now?" Melissa asked timidly.

"Absolutely not," the tall policeman told her. "I'm assuming those bicycles out there are yours. That's another law broken—riding around after dark without proper lights. And how about harassment?" He indicated

Crenshaw, who stood onstage with his bandmates. "This man was your Santa. He was there when you were in the Mug's Mug. And, surprise, surprise, here he is again—and here you are. You don't have to be Sherlock Holmes to figure out that you're stalking him." He addressed the hulking guitarist. "Sir, would you like to swear out a complaint against these young people?"

Griffin and the team regarded their former prime suspect fearfully. This could be real trouble. They may have been innocent of stealing the Star, but when it came to spying on Fingers Crenshaw, they were 1,000 percent guilty. If the police chose to look into it, they would find webcams around Crenshaw's apartment, microphones inside of it, and a tracker on his motorcycle.

The man they had worked so hard to expose as a crook had turned out to be blameless. And now he had the perfect opportunity to turn the tables on them.

Crenshaw shifted the guitar so his protruding belly rested on part of it. "All right, officer—they're annoying. I'll give you that. But, hey, they're just kids. Weren't you annoying when you were that age? Cut them some slack."

"They may be kids," Vizzini admitted grumpily, "but nobody in the department would characterize them as *just* kids. Are you sure you want to let them off the hook?"

"I know what it's like to get jammed up over a couple of bad decisions," the guitarist replied honestly.

"They're scared enough. Let them go." He punctuated this with a long rolling burp.

The team let out a subdued cheer that was silenced by Vizzini's scowl. "We're not done yet. You're all going to call your parents to come get you. And I'm going to have a little chat with them while we're together. Got it?" He turned to Mrs. Boucle and said, "You people go on with your party. We apologize for the interruption."

Tiffany looked at Logan and mouthed the words *I'm sorry.*

Encouraged, Logan beamed back at her. Obviously, his performance as someone who didn't hate Darren was having an impact.

Vizzini let out a long breath. "I think that covers everything—"

The words had not fully cleared his lips when a younger officer burst into the hall. "Sarge—call for backup! It's a killer—a monster—!"

With a roaring bark, Luthor bound past the terrified officer, plowed headlong through a throng of shocked partygoers, toppled a line of music stands, and settled himself at Crenshaw's feet.

"You see?" announced Savannah righteously. "Luthor is an excellent judge of character. He'd only give his loyalty to an innocent man."

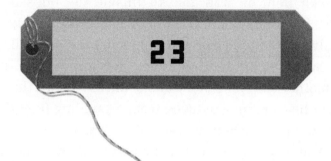

2 3

The fallout was brutal.

Once the parents gathered at the American Legion Hall, Detective Sergeant Vizzini read them the Cedarville Police Department version of the riot act. He finished with, "I don't have kids myself, so I don't pretend to be an expert and tell you folks how to raise yours. But if you've been waiting for the right time to show your children that actions have consequences, that opportunity is getting away from you. Whatever sermon or speech or punishment you've been holding back, use it now. I don't know if these kids are guilty or innocent, or to what degree. Either way, they're mixing themselves up in something that's way over their heads. I don't care if you have to tie them to their chairs. Keep them out of it!"

The parents took his advice to heart. Griffin, Pitch, Melissa, Savannah, and Logan were grounded until the end of vacation. Only Ben avoided this fate, because at this point, his parents were barely speaking to each other. Since all talk about his punishment had to pass through Ben, he was able to finagle the odds in his favor. He complained to his father that the family had finally started to celebrate Hanukkah big time, and now this would spoil it. Then he turned around and gave his mother the same story about Christmas. In the end, he got his sentence reduced from grounding to garbage takeout and clearing the table until April.

"And a fat lot of good it's going to do me," he muttered to Griffin over Skype. "Everybody I know is grounded, so I might as well be grounded, too. I haven't got anybody to hang out with except Ferret Face—and just try to have a conversation with him."

Pitch was informed that she would not be welcome on the family's next climbing trip. While the other Bensons tackled Lucifer's Claw in Alaska, she would spend the week on Grandma's farm in Kansas—the most horizontal place in the world. For Pitch, there could be no greater torture.

"Thanks a lot, Griffin!" she groused.

The Kellermans told Logan that even if the North Shore Players offered him a spot in their company, he would not be allowed to accept it. "And just when my pro-Vader strategy is finally making progress with Tiffany," he grumbled.

But Melissa's penalty turned out to be the harshest of all. In addition to her grounding, Mr. and Mrs. Dukakis removed every piece of technology—every computer, laptop, tablet, and phone—from her room. If it hadn't been for the new smartwatch she'd been building, she would have been completely cut off.

"I can't believe I'm being *punished*," the normally quiet girl raved over her homemade video-chat software, which was still in beta and provided a fuzzy picture and distorted sound. "I've hardly ever been punished in my entire life!"

Normally, her parents were so thrilled that their shy daughter had friends that they forgave her the ups and downs of Griffin's notorious plans. Apparently, that free ride had ended today. The Dukakises were furious.

"It's even worse for me," Savannah insisted on the six-way Skype call.

"How do you figure that?" growled Pitch. "You're just grounded, no bells and whistles. You're not missing out on two amazing trips in a row."

"When I'm grounded, my animals are grounded," Savannah explained. "Luthor needs room to roam; Cleopatra expresses her basic personality by exploring; even Lorenzo needs a little fresh air every now and then. Now they're all cooped up and it's my fault. How can I live with the guilt? It's the worst!"

"The worst is trying to climb in Kansas," Pitch amended in a colorless tone. "Even my grandma's house is a ranch with a flat roof. The only climbable thing was the windmill, but that came down in the last tornado."

"So you'll be bored for a week," snapped Logan. "My career is in ruins."

"I never knew my room would be so empty without technology," Melissa mourned. "They even took my autographed picture of Bill Gates."

"At least none of you guys have to be your family's personal message center," Ben put in bitterly. "'Ben, tell your father dinner's on the table.' 'Ben, tell your mother, "Broccoli again?"' 'Ben, tell your father no substitutions.' This from two people standing eight feet away from each other. It's murder."

Pitch snorted. "Big talk from Mr. I'm-Not-Grounded."

"I might as well be," Ben retorted. "I'm alone like a hermit, and my house can be seen from the International Space Station."

"Guys, this is going nowhere," Griffin interrupted. "I'm grounded, too, and longer than any of you. You don't have to tell me how much it stinks. But none of this will help get the plan back on track."

Although the team members weren't actually together, their reactions were identical—stony silence.

Uncharacteristically, it was quiet Melissa who spoke first. "Maybe it's my buggy software, but it sounded like you just said something about getting the plan back on track."

"Of course I did," Griffin confirmed. "Operation Starchaser isn't dead. Phase Two doubled down on Crenshaw, and that turned out to be a mistake. But that still leaves five suspects who may have taken the Star—Colchester's man Priddle, Miss Grier the neighbor, O'Bannon the electrician, Yvette Boucle the art professor, and Vader—you can never rule him out when something sleazy happens for money."

A babble of angry protest very nearly crashed the Skype connection.

Pitch was the loudest. "You're lucky we're all grounded, or we'd be on our way over to your place to kill you! There is no plan anymore, Griffin. You called Code Z, and now you're trying to uncall it! No way!"

"But how are we going to find out who stole the Star?" Griffin challenged.

"Simple," said Ben. "One day, maybe years from now, we'll open the newspaper and it'll say they caught the guy who did it. And then we'll know."

"That's not good enough!" Griffin was almost yelling. "We're under suspicion, and not just by the police. I know you get the dirty looks around town, same as me. Everyone thinks it's our fault that Santa's Workshop got shut down and now the Colchesters want to leave Cedarville. We're the Grinch, you guys! We stole Christmas and Hanukkah and the whole holiday season, and we're never going to be forgiven if we don't prove it. Not to mention that if Vizzini manages to pin it on us, we'll all end up in juvie."

"Vizzini *can't* pin it on us," Pitch countered. "We didn't do it, remember? So he'll never be able to find evidence that proves we did. As for people being mad at us, so what? They'll get over it. You know who won't get over it? Our parents, if we end up in any more trouble."

Savannah spoke up. "You know, last night at the Legion Hall, what if a nervous police officer had tried to hurt Luthor? Or worse, what if Luthor, in defending himself, had bitten someone. He could have been declared"—her voice cracked—"vicious! I don't want any part of this anymore."

"I'm sorry, Griffin," came Melissa's tiny voice. "I'm out, too. This whole punishment thing . . . I don't think I'm cut out for it. It's worse than the Blue Screen of Death."

"Same here," added Logan. "I have to put my career first."

"Thanks a million," Griffin said sarcastically. "Way to leave Ben and me holding the bag."

Ben shook his head. "You're on your own, Griffin. I've got enough trouble right here at home. Do you know that this year the first candle of Hanukkah comes on Christmas Eve? I'm afraid my house might lift off its foundation and blast away into hyperspace. I don't know why it hasn't happened already, with all the electricity we've been pumping through it. The last thing I can do is bring any more complications down on my family." Ferret Face appeared at his collar. "No, not you, little buddy. Mom and Dad."

Seated at the computer in his room, The Man With The Plan watched as, one by one, his friends signed off.

He was all alone.

And not just on the Skype screen.

24

The zipper wouldn't close.

Russell Colchester climbed up on the bed and sat directly on the lid of his suitcase, reaching underneath himself to finesse the zipper.

"I can get you another case."

The voice startled him. He looked to the doorway and saw his grandfather watching him. The old man's expression was deeply sad. Typical Grandpa. He'd been mooning around this place ever since he'd shut down his dumb Santa's Yawnfest.

"I'm good." He tried to force the zipper. It wouldn't budge.

"We have plenty of luggage," his grandfather renewed his offer. "Something larger, perhaps? You seem to need a little more space."

"Then I'd have to check it," Russell said firmly. "You're only supposed to carry on one bag."

Charles Colchester frowned. "One bag is all you have."

"Yeah—uh, right. I told you I stink at math."

His grandfather peered out the lead-paned balcony doors. A few flakes of snow danced in the air. "It looks as if we might have a white Christmas in the end."

"No!" Russell jumped off the suitcase and rushed to the window. "What if my flight gets canceled? They still fly in snow, right?"

"It depends how much snow," Grandpa replied in some amusement. "I keep forgetting that you're a California baby. Winter weather is a novelty to you."

Russell's eyes were fixed on the swirling flurries. "This is nothing, right? They can fly in this?"

"According to the weather forecast, they're expecting quite an accumulation. Eight inches at least."

"*Nooo!!*" Russell howled. "If the plane can't take off, then I'm stuck here for another whole day!"

Grandpa sighed. "I'm sorry you're so anxious to put an end to your time here. I'd been hoping that we would become closer."

Were all old people this sentimental, or was it a Long Island thing? Like the freezing cold made you want to huddle together for the body heat? Aloud, Russell said, "We *are* close, Grandpa. It's not our fault some jerk stole your Star and ruined everything."

"It wasn't all bad, I suppose," Mr. Colchester concluded. "At least you made a new friend."

"I did?"

"Young Darren Vader."

"Oh, right. Darren. Great kid. Now, about this

weather. Eight inches—that's not that much, right? How worried should I be . . . ?"

The Star of Prague gleamed down from every wall of the cramped faculty office. There were photographs large and small, artists' renderings, and even scientific diagrams done to scale with mathematical precision. Each exquisite star point measured exactly 20.4 centimeters in length; the outer globe had a diameter of 44.7 centimeters; the piece had a weight of 14.5 kilograms.

Yvette Boucle, professor of art history, sat back from her computer, gazing at the images around her as she collected her thoughts. She'd been working on her book about the Star for nearly two years now. She knew more about the piece than anyone in the world since the brilliant Bohemian artisan who'd created it. Certainly more than the Colchesters, who didn't appreciate the magnificent treasure they had—except as a topper for their annual Christmas tree.

Correction: The treasure they'd *once* had.

If only they'd allowed her to study it at close hand, everything might have been different.

She stood up and stretched. With the book so close to completion, the temptation was to work through the night. But this was Christmas Eve, and she belonged with her family.

On her way out, she double-locked her office door. She'd taken to doing that a lot lately, knowing that there was something precious inside.

Crossing the parking lot, she smiled as an ice-cold snowflake brushed the side of her cheek. Now it felt like Christmas. She couldn't wait to put the presents under the tree.

What Mrs. Boucle couldn't have known was that not all of her family would be waiting for her when she arrived home.

At that very moment, her daughter, Tiffany, was sneaking out of the house, closing the sliding door silently behind her.

The traffic was light, just as Priddle had expected. He was at the wheel of the Colchester Mercedes, tooling down the highway toward New York City.

Technically, he had the night off. But this was an important business transaction, worth a small fortune. If it had to be done on Christmas Eve, so be it.

He turned on his wipers as the snowfall on his windshield grew thicker and heavier. He certainly hoped he wasn't about to be caught in a blizzard.

But this was going to be worth it. No more would he have to put up with the drafty halls and crumbling plaster of a nineteenth-century mansion. No more would he have to suffer through the ancient plumbing and electrical failures. Best of all, he would have put on his last Holiday Spectacular, with its hordes of screaming, ungrateful, hyperactive, runny-nosed children.

After this deal went through, Priddle was moving up in the world.

He pressed harder on the accelerator.

The same snow that tickled Yvette Boucle's cheek and moistened Mr. Priddle's windshield had intensified as it began to collect on the roof of Mr. O'Bannon's brand-new truck.

He was parked on Shore Road, a quarter mile away from the Colchester property, just out of sight of the mansion, waiting for darkness to fall. It wouldn't be a pleasant walk in the blowing snow, but it was important for his purposes that he not be seen. The storm would help him with that. The accumulating powder would muffle his footsteps and fill in his tracks.

At last he decided the time was right. He cut the motor and got out of the truck, hefting a large pack. Then he removed a folding extension ladder from the back and began the now-slippery walk to the mansion, confident that he was not being observed.

His only worry was Miss Grier, the nosy neighbor. That old bat was like a one-woman CIA staked out right next door, minding the Colchesters' business. The Christmas spirit wouldn't stop her. Neither would a tsunami roaring up Long Island Sound.

But as he passed her home, he realized luck was with him. Her car was not in its usual place. She was out. He couldn't imagine anybody wanting to spend Christmas Eve with Miss Grier. But then again, look how he was spending it.

Of course, he had a very good reason.

He slipped in through the Colchesters' front gate, noting one garage door was open. The Mercedes was gone, but the limo and the Rolls were both there. That meant somebody was home, probably the old man and that sour-faced kid, plus a minimum staff. Mr. Colchester was kind enough to give most of the servants the night off.

He shouldered the ladder and backpack and ducked into the cover of the topiary garden. He had to stay hidden while he was doing what needed to be done. It would take time, but the payoff was going to be amazing.

The children looked nervous and uncertain as they met her at the door.

Miss Grier would never admit it, but she was none too confident herself. She didn't know these children from Adam. She'd never met their mother, and the last time she'd seen their father—her nephew—he'd been perhaps eleven or twelve, no bigger than the oldest of the kids.

"How do you do," Miss Grier greeted them formally. "I am your great-aunt Colleen."

The children shrank back a half step.

This was a bad idea, Miss Grier decided suddenly. These people were strangers to her. And the gift she'd brought them was far too extravagant and inappropriate. She shouldn't have come.

The invitation to spend Christmas Eve with the family had been a bolt out of the blue. Her first impulse had been to say no. Yet how could she? Miss Grier didn't get along very well with the rest of the world. Strangers or not, this nephew, his wife, and their three children were her only relatives.

Her nephew appeared—my, he'd grown into a handsome young man. "Kids, show Auntie the tree."

The three ran off into the small house, hollering for her to follow. Everything they did was at top speed—and top volume.

"In a minute," she called after them. "I need your father to help me get something out of the car." But they were already gone.

Her nephew embraced her. "We're so glad you're here."

"Children don't like me," she said stiffly.

"They'll like you," he assured her. "We're family."

"*You* never liked me."

He laughed. "Of course I did. I was just afraid of you. Now you sit and relax. I'll bring in the package for you."

"This is a two-person job," Miss Grier informed him. "It's heavy—and very fragile."

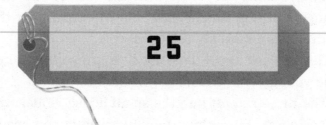

25

The snow falling around the Slovak house was multi-colored in the glow, and sizzled as it hit the hot lights.

It was Christmas Eve and the first candle of Hanukkah, so the dueling holiday displays were at their apex. The drei-dirigible swung in the wind of the oncoming storm, topping a kaleidoscope of luminescence, decoration, and music unmatched anywhere on the eastern seaboard. The house had been featured in several local newscasts, and pilots of night flights taking off from LaGuardia and Kennedy airports regularly pointed it out to their passengers.

Ben wasn't in a very festive mood. He sat in the kitchen, trying to feed a holiday dinner consisting of fruitcake and a potato latke to Ferret Face, who was having none of it.

Ben wasn't annoyed. On the contrary, he was proud. "That's right, little guy. Stand up for your rights as a carnivore."

The ferret seemed like a role model for Ben himself—someone who rejected having Christmas and Hanukkah shoved down his throat.

The sad part was Ben had always enjoyed both holidays—trimming the tree and lighting the menorah. And the presents; who didn't like presents? He'd never compared one against the other. A chocolate Santa tasted exactly the same as a coin of chocolate Hanukkah gelt once it was in your mouth.

His parents were in the living room, seated as far apart as humanly possible without actually falling off the opposite ends of the couch. Mom was watching *It's a Wonderful Life* on TV. Dad was ignoring that and reading a book on the life of Judah Maccabee, hero of the Hanukkah story. Even today, on the holiday itself—both holidays!—the competition was still on.

With me caught in the cross fire.

If only it was as easy as rejecting fruitcake and potato latke.

He needed air—a change of scenery—just for a little while. He'd never abandon his family on such a big night, but if he didn't clear his head, he was going to implode.

He stood up. "I'm going over to Griffin's."

Mrs. Slovak reached under the tree and pulled out a brightly wrapped pastry box. "Christmas cookies for the Bings," she explained.

He took it from her. "Got it."

"Wait!" Her husband rushed into the kitchen and

emerged with a paper plate covered with aluminum foil. "Latkes for the Bings," he announced proudly.

"Right." Ben balanced the plate atop the box.

"Not like that!" Mom complained. "The oil will drip down and spoil my cookies!"

"My latkes are not oily," Dad retorted icily. "They are light and fluffy."

"I can switch it." Ben placed the box over the plate. "It's fine. See?"

"Don't squash my latkes," his father warned.

And when Ben finally kicked into boots and stepped out into the cold, snowy evening, he felt like he'd just escaped a war zone.

He was grateful for his boots. The powdery snow was already up over his ankles and swirling around the streetlights. It was starting to look like they were going to get a whiter Christmas than anyone had bargained for.

The familiar walk to Griffin's house looked alien in the frosty landscape, but Ben's feet found their way by sheer force of habit, as they had so many times before.

Ferret Face poked his head out and tried to get his needle nose under the aluminum foil, but Ben flicked him away. "You already had your chance, mister. You snooze, you lose."

Mrs. Bing seemed surprised to find him on her doorstep. She hurried to hustle him in out of the storm. "Take a moment to warm up, but then I have to turn you around and send you home. Surely you know that Griffin is being punished."

Ben held out the box and plate in his arms. "Cookies and latkes from my folks. Happy holidays."

She took them. "Thanks, Ben. And my best to your parents. Your house is certainly . . . joyful this year." She looked torn as he turned for the door. "Oh, go on upstairs, just this once. It's Christmas Eve, after all."

"Am I ever glad to see you!" Griffin exclaimed as Ben let himself into the room. "I've never been grounded on vacation before. You don't even get out to go to school. It's like the state penitentiary!"

"The state penitentiary would be an improvement over my house these days," Ben said in a dispirited tone. "I had to escape, even for just a few minutes."

"Things aren't much better here," Griffin confided. "You know who called an hour ago? Mrs. Vader. She picked *today* to tell my dad that she can't file the patent for Fruit Armor yet—not till she has more proof that the invention really works. Merry Christmas, huh?"

"That's awful," agreed Ben. "What did your dad do?"

"What *could* he do? He went over to pick up his prototype so he can run some more tests on it. His holiday is totally ruined."

Ben gazed out Griffin's window toward the glow in the sky that he knew was coming from his own street. "There's a lot of that going around."

"This holiday was ruined the minute the Star of

Prague disappeared," Griffin said glumly. "And the worst part is we're just sitting on our butts letting it happen to us."

The bicycle was barely visible in the swirling snow as Tiffany Boucle plowed through the accumulating powder. It was a good thing she was riding a mountain bike, its wide tread biting into the drifts and propelling her forward. Otherwise, her progress would have been absolute zero. As it was, she was going to have to call Mom and Dad for a lift home. No way could she make it back from Cedarville to Green Hollow—not with this storm getting stronger. They were going to be mad, no question about that. But hopefully she'd have something to show them that was so fantastic that they would forgive her.

She turned onto Ninth Street—Cedarville's main drag—following the directions he had given her. The stores and businesses were all shut down for Christmas. The town was deserted. She checked her watch. She was late. She hoped he would understand and be waiting.

She remembered his description of the meeting place: *A hot-air balloon shaped like a four-sided top hanging over a house so lit up that it eclipses everything else in the neighborhood.*

There it was, hovering above the trees, just off to her left! She couldn't make out the exact shape through the falling snow, but it was flashing on and off. How many of those could there be? And there was no mistaking the eruption of light coming from below. This had to be the place!

She pedaled laboriously through the deepening powder, following the light in the sky. Partway there, riding became impossible, and she had to dismount and walk her bike. Ice crystals formed on her long lashes, almost blinding her. The wind nearly knocked her flat.

At last she rounded a corner to the house. She'd known it was coming, and even so, the sight of it close up took her breath away. It was beautiful . . . and hideous. Gorgeous . . . and tacky. Fabulous . . . and ridiculous. She couldn't decide what her real opinion was. But in any case, it was impressive that so many lights could fit on one little home.

And the music—chiming bells, Christmas carols, warring with very spirited violin solos. ·

She was so amazed by the sights and sounds that at first she didn't see him approaching.

"Tiffany—you came."

26

Mr. Bing didn't drive home so much as skid there. The station wagon slid down the block and into the driveway, where it came to a halt barely an inch from the garage door.

From Griffin's window, the boys watched him storming up the front walk. Then came the slam—and the yelling. Griffin had never heard his father so enraged.

"Oh, man, he sounds really steamed," whispered Ben.

Griffin put his finger to his lips and led his friend out of the room. The two stopped at the top of the stairs, snooping.

". . . bad enough that Daria Vader sits on my prototype for all this time and chooses *Christmas Eve* to throw it back in my face! Now she can't *find* it? That's not just irresponsible; it violates the trust between attorney and client! An invention that isn't patented yet can be pirated by anybody! It's her responsibility to keep it secure!"

Griffin and Ben exchanged a look of dismay. Fruit Armor was missing?

Mrs. Bing was alarmed. "Do you think it was *stolen*?"

"I don't know what to think!" he seethed. "It was in her basement. She swears it was there yesterday, but it's not there now!"

"Did the two of you look for it?" his wife probed.

"There was no time!" he cried in frustration. "Their precious spoiled brat of a son went out and he hadn't come back yet, so they had to go and look for him. Like a little snow could melt a big tank like him."

Griffin squeezed Ben's arm hard enough to splinter bone.

"Ow! What?"

"Vader's missing, too!" Griffin hissed. "Vader gone; Fruit Armor gone. There must be a connection."

"But what would Darren want with your dad's prototype?" Ben asked, mystified. "Besides using it to bounce off my head, I mean. Vader's probably not even missing. I'll bet he just went over to say good-bye to Russell and get in some last-minute butt-kissing before the kid takes off for California."

Griffin's concentration was so intense that the clunk of gears could almost be heard turning inside his head. The look was instantly recognizable to Ben. The Man With The Plan was working out a complicated problem.

He said, "Remember that round case for Dirk Crenshaw's disco ball? It always bugged me that it looked kind of familiar."

Ben was hopelessly lost. "What does a disco ball have to do with your dad's invention?"

Griffin's eyes were alight with discovery. "Don't you see? That case was exactly the size and shape of Fruit Armor! If the Star could fit inside that, then it could also fit inside—"

"Fruit Armor!" Ben finished in awe.

"That's why the police couldn't find the Star!" Griffin concluded triumphantly. "Vader's got it. And he hid it someplace no one would ever think to look— inside my dad's prototype!"

"Griffin and Ben!" came a harsh voice from below. "How dare you two eavesdrop on our private conversation?"

The boys looked down to find the Bings glaring up at them.

"Dad—you have to listen me!" Griffin exclaimed. "I think I know what happened to Fruit Armor!" Breathlessly, he stammered out the theory he had just shared with Ben.

"That's impossible," Mrs. Bing said flatly. "I know you and Darren don't get along, but to accuse him of this is pretty far-fetched. When the Star of Prague went missing, it was in all the papers and on TV. Everyone's looking for it—the police, private detectives hired by the Colchester family, insurance investigators—"

"I'll bet none of them ever looked in the Vaders' basement," Griffin insisted.

Mr. Bing stared at his son. Griffin was young and impetuous and stubborn and quick to jump to conclusions. But even when he wasn't exactly right, he was usually onto something. There was a good reason they called him The Man With The Plan.

"Get in the car," he ordered Griffin and Ben.

"Surely you're not taking this seriously?" his wife protested.

"Fruit Armor is missing. And this is the only lead I have."

Tiffany smiled when she recognized him under the ski mask. "Sorry I'm late, Logan. I was afraid you wouldn't wait for me."

Logan pulled up the mask. "Are you kidding? This is going to be awesome—to film you singing 'Winter Wonderland' with the snow falling all around you in front of the most festive house in town. Darren's going to love it," he added to win her over.

"I hope my parents do, too," she said nervously. "They aren't going to be too happy about me riding into the next town in the middle of a blizzard."

Logan frowned. "You didn't tell them?"

"You think they would have said yes?"

"I guess not, but . . ." He bit his lip. "You don't think your mom will blame it on me, do you?"

Tiffany looked around. "Where should I stand?"

"Right next to the inflatable snowman. And you'll

need this." He clipped a wireless microphone to the fur collar of her parka. "It'll boost your voice and trap out all the background music coming off the house."

She beamed at him as they crossed the street to the Slovaks' lawn. "Thanks so much, Logan. This is a really great idea."

"Hey, we performers have to support each other, right? Don't forget that part when you're talking to your mom."

Logan took out his phone and framed the camera shot.

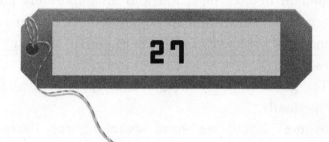

27

From: GBingPlanner
To: MountainGirl; AnimalsRUs; StageLogan;
TechWizard
ALERT: Vader has the Star hidden in Fruit Armor
prototype! Must be stopped at ALL COSTS!

At the Benson home, a second-story window opened and a shadowy figure swung a leg over the sill. The climb down the side of the house was effortless, despite the worsening storm. Pitch and her family had conquered some of the toughest mountains, crags, and rock faces in the world—for fun. A mere brick wall was child's play.

She wore no coat, so she was shivering as she dropped to the white-blanketed grass and rushed into the garage. A few moments later, the automatic door folded open and out she glided, in a full snowsuit and moving athletically on cross-country skis.

She skied around the corner, slowing down in front

of the Dukakis house. Her timing was perfect. Melissa, bundled in her warmest hat and an impossibly puffy down coat, let herself out a side door and came running.

She took in the sight of Pitch in all her alpine glory. "You ski, too?"

"I'm good at everything," Pitch explained, almost apologetically.

"Where should we start searching for Darren?" asked Melissa, jogging along beside the skier.

Pitch shrugged. "If you were a backstabbing slime-ball with ten million dollars' worth of loot, where would you be?"

"At the bank, probably," Melissa panted. "But they're closed now. Everybody is. It's Christmas."

"Yeah, you'd think even the crooks would be taking the night off. On the other hand, nobody ever went wrong thinking the worst of Vader. I guess we just cruise around and keep our eyes open. Anybody out on a night like this is bound to be up to no good, and that's got Darren written all over it."

Melissa pushed her curtain of hair under her hat to clear her vision for better searching.

Out of the swirling snow came a familiar barking. An enormous white dog exploded out of the storm and began to circle them.

A few seconds later, Savannah appeared, laughing. "Puppies love to roll in the snow."

"And what exactly does that have to do with Luthor?" Pitch asked.

"He's just a big baby at heart," Savannah explained. "Dogs are so in the moment. He probably doesn't even remember the last time he saw winter."

"Forget winter," Pitch interrupted. "When's the last time he saw Vader? That's the only reason I'm out here, freezing the end of my nose off."

"And we're all in big trouble if we get caught," Melissa put in. "We're supposed to be grounded, remember?"

"I feel Kansas closing in," Pitch groaned. "All right, I say we go street by street, tracking back and forth between here and the Vaders'. If he's still in town, we should spot him."

The Bings' station wagon had all-wheel drive, but still it skidded on the unplowed roads.

Griffin was in the passenger seat, staying as far from his father as possible without physically leaving the car. Mr. Bing's anger was so great that Griffin and Ben could feel it coming off him in waves of heat.

He verbalized his outrage in a running commentary: "Daria Vader, Attorney-at-Law—Daria Vader, Mother of Crook would be more like it! How could she leave *my* intellectual property at the mercy of her son the criminal? And she has the *nerve* to tell me I didn't do enough testing? It's good enough for her little brat to steal, isn't it . . . ?"

Griffin should have taken some satisfaction from his father's diatribe. He had spent years trying to convince his parents that Darren's money-grubbing dishonesty went far beyond simply "boys being boys." Yet now that the message had finally gotten through, he was too upset at his father's distress to reap any joy out of it. A major invention was at risk—not to mention a ten-million-dollar piece of art history.

Suddenly, Mr. Bing slammed on the brakes so hard that the car fishtailed, turning two complete revolutions on the icy road.

Ben sprawled out on the backseat, dumping Ferret Face onto the floor.

Griffin held on to the door for dear life. "Dad—what happened?"

"Weren't those your friends back there?"

Griffin became guarded. This was definitely not the time to confess that Operation Starchaser was still going on. "Why would my friends be out on a night like this?"

"Because I almost ran over Luthor! And wherever he is, the Drysdale girl is never far behind."

"Come on, Dad," Griffin coaxed. "Your invention is more important than a few kids and a dog. Let's keep searching."

"I'd love to," his father admitted. "But I can't let these kids freeze out here. We'll run them home and then come back out after Darren."

"They won't want to go," Griffin warned.

"I understand that," his father told him. "They're all grounded. Is there something in the Cedarville water that no kid ever obeys anything?"

He threw the station wagon into reverse and was just about to back up toward Griffin's friends when a loud motor shattered the quiet of the night. A fluorescent yellow snowmobile overtook them from behind and roared past.

Ben squinted. "Isn't that the Vaders' Ski-Doo?"

Even on this stormy night, it was impossible not to recognize the burly teenager seated at the controls. The glow of a streetlight illuminated the orange globe shape held in place between the wheel and his chest.

"My Fruit Armor!" Mr. Bing wheezed.

Rescuing the kids forgotten, the inventor took off after the snowmobile, honking his horn and yelling. He turned on his high beams just as Darren glanced over his shoulder. The fleeing boy was momentarily illuminated like a performer in a spotlight.

A hulking luxury SUV pulled even with the station wagon, and a crazed woman's voice bellowed, *"Darren, you come back here!"*

"It's the Vaders!" Griffin exclaimed. "They're after Darren, too!"

Seeing himself pursued by two larger, faster vehicles, Darren wheeled the Ski-Doo off the road in a spray of powder. He jounced through rock gardens and across lawns, tracing a path where the cars could not follow.

Savannah and Melissa were left far behind. The cars paralleled Darren on the street, but dared go no closer. Only Luthor galloped across front yards, leaping hedges and gaining on the snowmobile.

"Check it out," said Ben in surprise. "Luthor's an off-road vehicle!"

When Darren saw the big Doberman gaining on him, he twisted the throttle and the Ski-Doo burst forward. It leaped over a section of uneven ground, kicking up snow as it crunched back down again. Luthor blasted right through the cloud, never missing a stride. On the road, the two cars adjusted their speed to maintain pursuit.

"I can't believe Darren took the Star," remarked Ben, watching the chase from his spot in the backseat of the station wagon. "That's pretty awful, even for him."

"Are you kidding?" Griffin snorted. "I can't believe we ever bothered with another suspect once he was in the running."

Mr. Bing's hands were tight on the wheel. "Just so long as I get my prototype back."

"Darren, stop that!" Mrs. Vader's voice rang out. "It's not safe!"

Even if her son could have heard her over the Ski-Doo, her plea would not have changed his course of action. Hugging the Fruit Armor prototype to his chest, he gunned the engine to full power and rocketed forward.

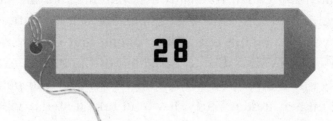

28

*S*leigh bells ring, are you listening . . . ?"

Logan was vibrating with excitement, but he forced himself to hold his phone steady as the camera recorded Tiffany's performance. She was great, of course, but the setting was even better. The swirling snow in the air, the sparkling drifts on the ground. Not even Steven Spielberg could have set up such a perfect shot. Tiffany was singing about a winter wonderland in the middle of the ultimate winter wonderland.

But the pièce de résistance was the Slovak house in the background. The Santas and the dreidels; the reindeer and the fiddler; the snowmen and the menorah; the wreaths and the latkes—all lit up in a shimmering explosion of brilliant color. It was so glaringly bright that the light meter read FULL SUN in the middle of the night. And that didn't even include the drei-dirigible, which hovered over the roof, out of frame.

The video had to be perfect, since Mrs. Boucle was going to see it. And, Logan reflected, his elation dimming a little, she was pretty angry right now. Before filming, Tiffany had called to assure her parents that she was okay, and to ask for a ride home. Even at a distance, the yelling coming out of her phone had been pretty scary. Logan was sure to get some of the blame, especially since Mrs. Boucle was still sore over the police raid on her holiday party. It would take a stellar video, with the potential to go viral on YouTube, to undo all that damage and earn him a chance to get into the North Shore Players.

The roar came suddenly, approaching fast. It sounded like a power mower, only louder. Logan had a split second to worry that the noise might penetrate the microphone's sound filter and spoil the video.

Then the Ski-Doo was upon them.

Logan jumped one way, Tiffany the other, as the big machine plowed through. The spinning treads kicked a powerful stream of snow into Logan's face, blinding him momentarily. When at last he was able to clear his vision, an even more terrifying sight met his eyes— Luthor, at point-blank range, bearing down on him in full flight.

He managed to gasp "Stay low!" to Tiffany before planting his face back into the snow. He could feel the one-hundred-fifty-pound Doberman using his back as a launch pad as he hit the Slovaks' lawn at warp speed. He took out the inflatable snowman first, blasting clear through it, popping it like a soap bubble. As the big dog thundered across the lawn, his powerful legs got caught up in the guy wires anchoring the largest, brightest, and most elaborate Christmas and Hanukkah display on Long Island.

Long strings of multicolored lights were ripped from the walls, exploding in showers of sparks. Down off the roof came the sleigh, the reindeer, Santa, and all his elves. The big menorah dissolved in a fireball, taking the spinning dreidels with it. Bulbs burst; wreaths burned; latkes melted. Holly and mistletoe rained from above.

The bells ceased to peal. The carols halted in mid-hallelujah. The klezmer music fell silent.

"Dude!" Griffin said in awe. "Your house!"

Ben could only look on in horror.

There was a low crackling sound as the fiddler on the roof began to lean dangerously over the eaves. Below it stood Tiffany, frozen with fear.

Logan came out of nowhere, diving like an NFL linebacker. He hit her at the knees, knocking her backward, sending the two of them rolling one over the other through the snow. The fiddler plunged into the space they had occupied a split second before. It made virtually no sound as it shattered into a million pieces.

With a final lunge that snapped the wire, sending the drei-dirigible soaring toward the heavens, Luthor hurled himself onto the fleeing Ski-Doo. One instant, Darren's eyes were scanning the snow-covered lawns that lay ahead, plotting his escape route; the next, his entire field of vision was filled with dog.

Panicking, he yanked on the controls, hoping to dislodge the terrifying animal. He succeeded all too well. In a tremendous spray of snow, the Ski-Doo flipped over on its side. Luthor and Darren were thrown free. If it hadn't been for the fresh powdery drifts, both would have been knocked silly. As it was, Darren was flung into a bush and came up sputtering with a mouthful of slush.

He looked around in dismay, taking frantic stock. There was the mutt; there was the Ski-Doo. Where was . . . ?

Then he spotted it. The Fruit Armor prototype was bouncing like a giant orange soccer ball across the snowy lawn toward—

"Not the road!" he howled.

Mr. Bing slammed on the brakes and the station wagon lurched to a halt. But the Vaders' SUV sped past it and hit the prototype head-on. It sailed high through the air, struck a metal light pole with a resounding *bong*, and dropped like a stone.

"Nooo!" Darren got up and sprinted toward it.

Mr. Bing leaped out of his car and began a high-stepping slog through the snow. Griffin and Ben were hot on his heels. Mr. and Mrs. Vader left their dented SUV in the middle of the street and joined the race.

As the group converged on the battered prototype, a stretch limousine skidded around the corner from the opposite direction and fishtailed to a stop in front of the Slovak house. The passenger door opened and a slight figure jumped out and picked up the Fruit Armor globe.

"Russell?" chorused Griffin and Ben.

"Darren, you smashed it!" Russell Colchester accused. "I told you to take good care of it!"

"I did!" Darren babbled. "I mean—I tried! I mean"—he pointed a gloved finger accusingly at Luthor—"that monster jumped on me!"

His face pink with emotion and windburn, Mr. Bing ran to his invention and snatched it away from Russell. "This prototype is not yours."

"Yeah, but what's inside it is his!" Darren blurted.

His mother rushed up and grabbed him by both shoulders. "What *is* inside it, Darren?"

Darren turned almost as white as the snow. "Oh, hi, Mom," he said faintly. "Crazy weather, huh?"

His mother would not be distracted. *"What's inside that Fruit Armor?"*

Russell was despondent. "It doesn't matter. It's in a million pieces now."

Mr. Bing popped the lock on his invention, took out the inner globe, and separated the two halves. He removed the contents and held them up for all to see.

The gleam of the streetlight found it first, and it shone brighter than the Slovak house ever had, its outer shell flawless and clear, its ancient stained-glass star as multicolored and magnificent as the day it had been created in eleventh-century Bohemia.

"I was right!" breathed Griffin.

"The Star of Prague!" cried an awed voice behind him in equal measures of reverence and excitement. It was Yvette Boucle. She and her husband had arrived to rescue their daughter just in time to see the Slovaks' holiday display meet its spectacular pyrotechnic end.

"It's okay!" Russell was astounded. "How come it's not broken? It fell off a speeding snowmobile! It got hit by an SUV! It bounced off a metal pole!"

Mr. Bing was triumphant. "Things don't get broken when they're inside Fruit Armor." He turned meaningful eyes on his patent attorney. "If it can protect thousand-year-old stained glass, think what it can do for a bushel of peaches."

If Daria Vader received his message, she gave no indication. Her full attention was focused on her son. "Darren, are you crazy? Why would you steal a priceless art treasure?"

"I didn't steal it!" Darren pointed at Russell. "*He* stole it! I just hid it for him. I was on my way to meet the limo so he could take it to the airport and fly it to California."

Russell drew himself up to his full height and assumed a haughty look that oozed thirteen years of wealth and privilege. "I didn't steal it. I'm a Colchester. It belongs to me. I heard O'Bannon warning about water leaking down to the electrical box, so I used the hose to make it happen. When the lights went out, I ran to the top of the stairs, grabbed the Star, and stashed it in the attic above my closet. Who was going to suspect me? And when all those detectives and insurance people started searching more carefully, I smuggled it over to Darren's and we hid it in the invention."

"But *why*?" Darren's father pleaded. "Why would you cause your grandfather so much suffering?"

"All I wanted was to go home to California. And I knew he'd never let me, so long as that stupid Santa's Workshop was still on. So I shut it down. I would have given him back his Star. What's the point of keeping it? It'll be mine eventually."

"But it's not yours *yet*," Mrs. Vader said harshly. "And now you're going to take it back to your grandfather and confess what you did."

Russell shot her a self-assured smile. "No can do, Mrs. V. I've got a plane to catch."

Everyone laughed.

"I guess you're not used to our northeast weather, Russell," Mr. Bing informed him. "All the airports are shut down tight. You're spending Christmas in Cedarville, whether you like it or not."

All the color drained out of Russell's face.

Pitch snowplowed up, raising a cloud of powder with her skis. "What happened?" She took in the sight of the Star of Prague in Mr. Bing's arms, and the darkened Slovak home, now bare of any decoration. The wreckage of the dueling Christmas-versus-Hanukkah displays lay in the snowy yard, some of it sparking and sizzling. "Oh, man, I always miss the good stuff!"

"Where are the others?" asked Griffin.

"On their way," Pitch reported. "About a block back."

As if on cue, a distant call sounded. "Luthor—sweetie! I'm coming."

The big Doberman leaped to his feet, shook the snow off his coat, and rushed off to find Savannah, barking all the way.

Logan and Tiffany, frosted from head to toe, joined the group. Mr. Boucle enfolded his daughter in a huge bear hug.

"I'm sorry, Daddy," she warbled. "I just wanted to make you and Mom a video for Christmas."

Mrs. Boucle rounded on Logan, her entire body trembling with emotion. "I saw what you did," she rasped.

"I didn't mean it!" Logan backed away. "Please don't kill me!"

Tears began streaming down her cheeks. "You saved our daughter's life. You risked your own safety to push her away from that falling fiddler! You're a hero! And if you still want a place with the North Shore Players, you've got it!"

It was the kind of miracle that only happened during the holidays.

29

When Mr. O'Bannon finally knocked on the front door of the mansion, it took a long time for anyone to answer. Most of the staff had the night off to enjoy Christmas Eve. When at last the intricately carved oak portal swung open, Charles Colchester himself was standing behind it.

"Mr. O'Bannon," he said in surprise. "Why aren't you at home with your family?"

"I'm heading there right now," the electrician promised, "but there was something important I had to do first."

In each hand, he held the end of a long extension cord. He connected the cables and something amazing happened.

The property lit up. Strings of white lights had been woven through the trees that lined the front lawn, spelling out the message:

MERRY X-MAS MR. C

"I get that it's been a rough holiday for you, sir, and you might not feel like celebrating. But you should know that the people of this town admire and respect you. And we always will."

Charles Colchester stared at the display that this workingman had done on his own time out of the goodness of his heart. He took a handkerchief from his pocket and began to dab at tear-filled eyes.

"Thank you," he said in a husky voice. "This means more than you'll ever know. And Merry Christmas to you and your family."

The telephone rang. Mr. Colchester turned and picked up the receiver on the hall table. As the old man listened, his face paled to an unhealthy shade of gray. "And you're absolutely certain of this? . . . I see . . . Thank you for telling me. I'll come at once."

"Are you all right?" the electrician asked anxiously.

Mr. Colchester seemed to have aged twenty years in the course of that thirty-second call. "The Star of Prague has been recovered."

"That's great news—isn't it?"

"It was my own grandson who took it. And now I have the task of informing the police that I'm not pressing charges—which is the only reason why Russell won't be arrested."

At that moment, Mr. O'Bannon would not have traded places with this multimillionaire for all his great wealth. "I've got my truck down the block," he offered gently. "I can give you a lift to pick him up."

"Thank you. Just give me a moment to call Priddle. I sent him into the city to buy a penthouse for me. I was going to sell out and leave Cedarville forever." The old man shook his head. "That would have been the biggest mistake of my life."

Christmas Eve was magical for Miss Grier. She couldn't believe she'd ever considered declining this invitation. What a crotchety old bird she'd turned into! She needed to socialize more.

People would keep her young. *Children* would keep her young.

She held out as long as she could. But after two hours she gave in to the burning glances that her grandniece and grandnephews were casting in the direction of the large gift she had brought.

"All right," she said. "Let's open it, shall we?"

The present turned out to be a seventy-five-inch curved ultra-HD TV for the whole family. It generated such excitement that Christmas Eve was put on hold so her nephew could set it up right away.

There were oohs and aahs as the huge picture came into focus. It was a live video feed. The headline across the top of the screen declared:

BREAKING NEWS—UFO OVER NYC

"What on earth?" exclaimed Miss Grier.

A spotlight shone through the blowing snow of the

blizzard, illuminating what looked like some sort of hot-air balloon flying over the spires of the Manhattan skyscrapers.

"It must be Santa in his sleigh!" crowed the youngest nephew.

"No way," scoffed his older sister. "I'll bet it's an alien space probe!"

"I'm sure it's nothing more than a weather balloon," their mother soothed.

And then the side of the flying object lit up with the message HAPPY HANUKKAH.

"We have new information coming in," reported the news anchor. *"The air force has identified the UFO as a drei-dirigible, a common Hanukkah decoration. I repeat—the UFO is totally harmless. There is no cause for alarm . . ."*

"It isn't Santa," the youngest nephew complained, disappointed.

"But it *will* be," his great-aunt assured him. "Santa only comes when you're asleep."

Ben let himself in the front door and stomped the snow off his boots.

"Oh, you're back," said his mother, who was still watching television.

"How is it out there?" added Dad, glancing up from his book about Judah Maccabee.

Ben stared. Was it possible that they hadn't noticed what had happened to their own house? Were they so fixed on tuning out each other that they'd tuned out everything else?

"There's a lot of snow on the ground," he told them. "And . . . other stuff."

"Benjamin, what are you talking about?" Estelle Slovak asked.

There was no point in dragging it out. "Mom, Dad— put your coats on. You'd better see this."

He led them outside, and the Slovaks began to take in the scope of the wreckage—ruined reindeer, charred dreidels, half a Santa, a shattered fiddler, the tattered remains of a snowman, a melted mess that only slightly resembled a menorah, shredded holly, spaghetti strings of burnt-out lights, latkes scattered over a broken sleigh.

A single red light remained—Rudolph's nose, detached from its owner at the end of a scorched wire. They watched as it flickered and died.

Ben held his breath during the long silence that followed. Even Ferret Face poked his needle nose outside, as if awaiting their reaction.

"You know," Mr. Slovak said finally, "I think the house looks better this way."

His wife nodded slowly. "I couldn't agree more."

When they walked back inside, husband and wife were holding hands.

30

Cedarville's Santa's Workshop Holiday Spectacular officially reopened its doors on December 27.

Never before in its 158-year history had the Colchester mansion seen such crowds. The entire town of Cedarville was there, and many who had come from much farther afield. News of the disappearance of the famous Star of Prague had spread all around the Northeast. Now that it was back again, everyone wanted to see it.

Miss Grier threw her property open to provide parking for so many extra visitors. It was a stunning change of heart for an unfriendly neighbor who had spent so many holidays on the phone with the police, demanding that illegally parked cars be towed away. Even more amazing, she brought her grandnephews and grandniece to reopening night. It was the first time she'd set foot inside the Colchester home after living next door to it for more than sixty years.

"I guess the holiday spirit just got to me this season," she told everybody.

The Star of Prague was once again in its rightful place atop the towering Christmas tree in the teeming Great Hall. It had been examined by a museum curator, a glass expert, and Mrs. Boucle. All three declared it undamaged and 100 percent good as new despite its trials and tribulations inside Fruit Armor.

Another piece of good news: Mrs. Vader decided that the events of Christmas Eve were all the testing the new invention would need. Mr. Bing was on the fast track to another patent.

"Quit scratching, Ferret Face!" Ben complained. "I know the shirt's tight. I don't like it any more than you do!"

Now that the Holiday Spectacular was on again, Santa's Elves were back on the job—and back in costume, complete with tunics, tights, vests, jingling slippers, and pointed ears. She stormed off, ear points held high.

"Yeah, thanks a lot, Griffin," Pitch growled. "It didn't say anywhere in Operation Starchaser that when it was all over, we'd have to be elves again. Some Man With The Plan you are."

"At least we're not grounded anymore," Melissa put in optimistically.

"*I* was never grounded in the first place," grumbled Ben, reaching inside his tunic in an attempt to shift Ferret Face into a more comfortable position.

"All right, you guys," Griffin told them. "It stinks to be elves again. I get that. But you have to admit it could be a lot worse. Is Detective Sergeant Vizzini still bugging us? No. Does the entire town hate us because we ruined Christmas? No again. I'd say this plan was a pretty big success."

"It worked out for me," Logan agreed. "If all this hadn't happened, I never would have gotten into the North Shore Players. Mrs. Boucle hated my guts."

"Smart lady," Darren approved. "You have very hateable guts. I hate them, too."

Tiffany turned on him. "You shut your big mouth, Darren Vader! Logan is ten times the person you'll ever be! You're lucky you're not in jail right now! You and Russell Colchester—who's the only reason you're the *second*-worst person in the world, instead of number one! I'm *glad* they sent him away to California. If I had my way, they would have sent him to the moon, and you with him!"

Since Mr. Colchester never pressed charges against his grandson for stealing the Star, Darren was off the hook, too. It was impossible to be an accomplice to a crime that had never been committed. Now his only problems were angry parents and an even angrier Tiffany Boucle. He didn't much care that she no longer had a crush on him, but it annoyed him to no end that she had transferred her affections to Logan. Wherever the young actor went in the Great Hall, Tiffany followed with the same wide-eyed worshipful look she had once reserved for Darren.

"You've got the plan to thank for that, too," Griffin reminded Logan. "Tiffany ditched Vader and now she's totally into you."

"I'm going to have to find a way to let her down easy," reflected Logan with a world-weary smile. "I don't have time for a girlfriend. My most important relationship is with my acting. Although," he mused, "shooting music videos with Tiffany got me thinking. Acting's okay, but what I'd really like to do is *direct*."

A resounding *"Ho, ho, ho!"* boomed through the Great Hall.

Santa Claus made his way through the crush, handing out candy canes, his loyal reindeer at his side—Luthor, with the papier-mâché antlers tied to his massive head.

Dirk Crenshaw was back, as ever the perfect Santa. Savannah beamed, watching her dog reunited with his friend. "I'm so happy for Luthor!"

"Why Luthor?" asked Ben. "You should be happy for Crenshaw. He's the one getting all that money."

It was true. Mr. Colchester had offered a reward for information leading to the recovery of his Star. Griffin and the team had decided to pass on their prize to Dirk Crenshaw to help pay off his gambling debts and to get his life back on track.

Part of their decision came from a group feeling of guilt over how they'd falsely suspected this man and trailed his footsteps around town. In their minds, they had tried and convicted him, when all the while he was innocent. Yet when Vizzini had offered him the chance to press charges against them, he'd said no.

His exact words had been: *I know what it's like to get jammed up over a couple of bad decisions.* Crenshaw had let the team off the hook for *their* bad decision to spy on him. Now it was their turn to return the favor. Too well Griffin remembered Gustave, the bodybuilder debt collector from that night in the old tennis racket factory. Crenshaw might have been a none-too-friendly cigar-smoking slob with stomach gas to spare, but nobody deserved Gustave.

Savannah saw it differently. In her opinion, the reward should have gone to Luthor, since he'd been the one who'd leaped on the snowmobile and stopped the fleeing Darren. And there was no question that Luthor would have wanted to give his money to the front man of Fingers and the Flytraps.

An added bonus of donating their prize to Crenshaw—it drove Darren absolutely crazy.

"You guys are such morons!" he lamented. "It's like flushing cold, hard cash down the toilet! Why didn't you just give it to *me*?"

Pitch laughed in his face. "You really dream in Technicolor, Vader. Not only did you do nothing to earn this reward. You were part of the reason they had to offer one in the first place!"

"Hey, I didn't steal anything," Darren defended himself. "I just helped out a friend. Sue me for doing exactly what we used to sing songs about in kindergarten!"

"*We* can't sue you," Griffin informed him. "Mr. Colchester can. And he might still try if we tell him about this conversation."

"Okay, fine," Darren sulked. "I don't deserve any money. But why Crenshaw, huh? Why a random hobo in a Santa suit?"

"That shows what *you* know," Savannah retorted. "Dirk has to be a wonderful person, or Luthor wouldn't love him."

That evening, just before the mansion had opened its doors, Santa had gathered all the elves together in the Workshop for a heartfelt thank-you. Everyone got a hug, even Darren. It smelled of motor oil, tobacco, and five-alarm chili. Ferret Face found it appetizing, and Ben had to hold the little creature in place inside the elf costume.

"I can't believe you kids did this for me," Crenshaw said earnestly. "You barely know me."

The team members flushed. Because of listening devices, webcams, GPS trackers, e-mail hacking, and a whole lot of personal surveillance, they knew Dirk Crenshaw better than his own mother did.

"This is the nicest thing that's ever happened to me. I swear I'll pay you back if it's the last thing I do."

Savannah tried to explain about animals being excellent judges of character, but Crenshaw cut her off with another one of his thunderous belches.

"Five minutes ago," he went on, "Mrs. Boucle hired me as the musical director for the North Shore Players. It was the faith you kids showed in me that gave me the confidence to apply for that job. It made all the difference." And the hugging started over again.

So when the great doors opened to admit the crowd, Santa and his elves were in tears.

Charles Colchester interpreted this to be an emotional reaction to the reopening of the Holiday Spectacular. "I cherish this town!" he exclaimed hoarsely.

Priddle put an arm around Crenshaw's shoulder and faced the elves. "It's probably well known that I don't much like children. But I could make an exception for you lot. You're very kind young people—and you're even more resourceful than you are kind." He scowled at Darren. "Except for you."

It was the best Holiday Spectacular anyone—even Mr. Colchester himself—could remember. It lasted until nearly midnight, and Griffin and Ben stayed after that to help clean up and prepare to do it all again tomorrow.

Priddle sent the chauffeur to drive them home in the Colchester limo.

They approached Ben's house first, where a Dumpster sat on the driveway, piled high with debris from the dueling holiday displays.

"Wow." Griffin whistled. "That's a lot of junk. You don't think your folks will go nuts and do it all again next year, do you?"

Ben shook his head. "No way. It used to drive my dad bananas that Hanukkah always took a backseat to Christmas. But did you hear where the drei-dirigible ended up when it finally came down? It landed right on top of the big Christmas tree in Rockefeller Center."

Griffin was wide-eyed. "No way!"

"So for about an hour, until the sanitation department could bring in the cherry picker to take it down, it said 'Happy Hanukkah' on top of the most famous Christmas tree on the planet. Yeah, I think Dad got it out of his system. Trust me."

The Man With The Plan was speechless . . . which might have been the biggest holiday miracle of all.

About the Author

Gordon Korman's first Swindle mysteries were *Swindle, Zoobreak, Framed, Showoff, Hideout, Jackpot,* and *Unleashed.* His other books include *Slacker, This Can't Be Happening at Macdonald Hall!* (published when he was fourteen); *The Toilet Paper Tigers; Radio Fifth Grade;* the trilogies Island, Everest, Dive, Kidnapped, Titanic, and The Hypnotists; and the series On the Run. He lives in New York with his family and can be found on the Web at www.gordonkorman.com.